THE LEGACY SERIES

SERIES TITLES

All Gone Now
Michael Caleb Tasker

This Is How We Speak
Rebecca Reynolds

I Felt My Life With Both My Hands
Jessica Treadway

Hands
Pardeep Toor

Lafferty, Looking for Love
Dennis McFadden

All That It Seems
Jim Landwehr

Your Place in This World
Jake La Botz

Apple & Palm
Patricia Henley

Bodies in Bags
Jamey Gallagher

A Green Glow on the Horizon
Dawn Burns

How We Do Things Here
Matt Cashion

Neon Steel
Jennifer Maritza McCauley

Release of Information
Kali White VanBaale

The Divide
Evan Morgan Williams

Yes, No, I Don't Know
Kathryn Gahl

The Price of Their Toys
John Loonam

The Caged Man
Calvin Mills

A Day Doesn't Go By When I Don't Have Regrets
J. Malcolm Garcia

These Are My People
Steve Fox

We Should Be Somewhere by Now
Stephen Tuttle

Burner and Other Stories
Katrina Denza

The Plan of Chicago
Barry Pearce

Trust Issues
K.P. Davis

Adult Children
Laurence Klavan

Guardians & Saints
Diane Josefowicz

Western Terminus: Stories and A Novella
Michael Keefe

Like Human
Janet Goldberg

The Hopefuls
Elizabeth Oness

Never Stop Exiting
Michael Hopkins

Broken Heart Syndrome
Anne Colwell

The Mexican Messiah: A Novella & Stories
Jay Kauffmann

Close to a Flame
Colleen Alles

American Animism
Jamey Gallagher

Keeping What's Best Left Kept Secret
David Ricchiute

Soaked
Toby LeBlanc

The Path of Totality
Marie Zhuikov

Shocker in Gloomtown
Dan Libman

The Continental Divide
Bob Johnson

The Three Devils and Other Stories
William Luvaas

The Correct Response
Manfred Gabriel

Welcome Back to the World: A Novella & Stories
Rob Davidson

Greyhound Cowboy and Other Stories
Ken Post

Close Call
Kim Suhr

The Waterman
Gary Schanbacher

Signs of the Imminent Apocalypse and Other Stories
Heidi Bell

What We Might Become
Sara Reish Desmond

The Silver State Stories
Michael Darcher

An Instinct for Movement
Michael Mattes

The Machine We Trust
Tim Conrad

Gridlock
Brett Biebel

Salt Folk
Ryan Habermeyer

The Commission of Inquiry
Patrick Nevins

Maximum Speed
Kevin Clouther

Reach Her in This Light
Jane Curtis

The Spirit in My Shoes
John Michael Cummings

The Effects of Urban Renewal on Mid-Century America and Other Crime Stories
Jeff Esterholm

What Makes You Think You're Supposed to Feel Better
Jody Hobbs Hesler

Fugitive Daydreams
Leah McCormack

Hoist House: A Novella & Stories
Jenny Robertson

Finding the Bones: Stories & A Novella
Nikki Kallioy

Self-Defense
Corey Mertes

Where Are Your People From?
James B. De Monte

Sometimes Creek
Steve Fox

The Plagues
Joe Baumann

The Clayfields
Elise Gregory

Kind of Blue
Christopher Chambers

Evangelina Everyday
Dawn Burns

Township
Jamie Lyn Smith

Responsible Adults
Patricia Ann McNair

Great Escapes from Detroit
Joseph O'Malley

Nothing to Lose
Kim Suhr

The Appointed Hour
Susanne Davis

PRAISE FOR
All Gone Now

The emotionally spare yet evocative stories in Michael Caleb Tasker's *All Gone Now* smolder with tension. From the night cafés of New Orleans to the empty highways of New Mexico, we meet burnt-out bull riders, nightmare-haunted prize fighters, and beguiling strangers who aren't what they seem. These stories call to mind Ernest Hemingway, Carson McCullers, and Patricia Highsmith—but with a peculiar, moody magic that's all Tasker's own.

—JOANNA PEARSON
author of *Bright and Tender Dark*

Tasker writes fiction like a vivid literary dream that lingers long after the last line. He brings to life the wounded and the lost, and the yearning within the human heart, with a tender attention to detail and a sublime grasp of character.

—MICHAEL SALA
author of *The Restorer*

All Gone Now is a masterful and affecting collection that finds spooky beauty in trains and cafes, rodeos and circuses, in motel scotch and cigarette smoke. In road stories that range from the Gulf Coast to Canada, restless men and women linger at windows, with a sad gaze as in Hopper paintings, but this book is sad in the best way. Music plays behind many scenes and there is also lovely music in the intense lyrical prose.

—MARK ANTHONY JARMAN
author of *Burn Man*

ALL GONE NOW

stories

Michael Caleb Tasker

CORNERSTONE PRESS
UNIVERSITY OF WISCONSIN-STEVENS POINT

Cornerstone Press, Stevens Point, Wisconsin 54481
Copyright © 2026 Michael Caleb Tasker
www.uwsp.edu/cornerstone

Printed in the United States of America.

Library of Congress Control Number: 2026931954
ISBN: 978-1-968148-44-7

All rights reserved.

This is a work of fiction. Names, characters, businesses, places, events, and incidents are either the products of the author's imagination or used in a fictitious manner. Any resemblance to actual persons, living or dead, or actual events is purely coincidental.

Cornerstone Press titles are produced in courses and internships offered by the Department of English at the University of Wisconsin–Stevens Point.

DIRECTOR & PUBLISHER	EXECUTIVE EDITORS
Dr. Ross K. Tangedal	Jeff Snowbarger, Freesia McKee
EDITORIAL DIRECTOR	SENIOR EDITORS
Brett Hill	Paige Biever

PRESS STAFF
Samantha Bjork, Sophie McPherson, Andrew Bryant, Eleanor Belcher, Natalie Daute, Lilly Kulbeck, Oliver McKnight, Grady Roesken, Sam Zajkowski, Madison Schultz, Autumn Vine

To Katerina

stories

The Wrong Side of Gone	1
The Luckiest Man in Town	18
All Gone Now	31
Nothing Shaking	49
Clear Midnight	63
Mount to the Sky	80
Some Kind of Heaven	97
Muddle Through	112
Enough for a Stranger	134
Innocent	148
Cracked Bells	166
Acknowledgments	183

Let them think what they liked, but I didn't mean to drown myself. I meant to swim till I sank—but that's not the same thing."

—Joseph Conrad, "The Secret Sharer"

The Wrong Side of Gone

She left El Paso early. Eight lanes of empty highway and the only other car on the road came straight at her, slowly, almost thoughtfully, the tired tangerine sun slipping over the mountains behind it. The car swayed a little, waking with the world, and then turned in an easy U and drove away. Dawn kept on coming and she drove north, crossed into New Mexico, and thought she could still smell the cigarettes and sadness from his last hard hug.

She stopped at Denny's for breakfast and watched the neon sign from the motel across the highway flicker at her. When the lights changed the painted cowboy lay down to sleep. He made it look good, she thought, made it look easy, like the second his head touched the pillow he would roll away into tender dreams. The waitress brought her coffee and toast and Dusty smiled up at her, sure she had seen her somewhere before. The waitress smiled back with eyes so blue they looked like they had spent too many years staring into that high and hollow desert sun.

While she ate she watched the painted cowboy sleep. She thought the burning neon blue of his pillow looked like the ocean.

By noon she was back home. Her mother was out front, drinking coffee, leaning against the railing just so, talking to Shawn, making his mouth water. Dusty sat in the car, waiting for the wind. She wondered how her mother always got her hair so pretty. When Shawn walked away Dusty got out of the car, went up to the porch and sat on the step. Her mother sat down next to her.

"Hey, baby."

"You smell good."

"New perfume," her mother said. "Am I wearing too much?"

"Yeah. A little. But it's good."

"How was Lewis?"

"Still the same."

"He meet anyone yet?"

"Not that he mentioned."

"He ask about me?"

"Yeah."

"What'd he say?"

"*How's Jo?*"

"That's it?"

"That's it."

Her mother leaned against her. She was warm. There was the smell of a cigarette smoked long ago.

"You work tonight?" Jo asked.

"No. Not 'til morning. Not 'til five."

"Good," Jo said. "I don't like you working those night shifts."

The sky was clear; blue and wide and hot and she thought it was good weather for snakes. Shawn came out of the manager's office carrying a six-pack of beer and went into his unit, careful not to look at anyone, and slid his door closed and the curtain too. She could hear kids in the swimming pool. Sweat ran down from her hairline and she tried to remember the last time it rained.

It was still dark when she woke. Something was burning out in the desert and she could see the far away flicker of dancing embers from her bedroom window. She dressed quietly, careful not to wake her mother, and when she left she listened a minute at her door and felt that heavy warmth in the air and knew someone was with her. When she drove away she saw the television light twitching at Shawn's windows and his door was open. She could smell that fire, out in the desert, burning away, the smoke rolling in on the cool, lazy wind. She turned onto the highway. There was a touch of lonesome purple light in the sky.

When she got to Hondo's she unlocked the gas pumps and turned on the lights. The store smelled of dead air, of Styrofoam and reheated food, and she left the doors open and when she finished mopping dawn had crawled its way into the sky so that the purple light seemed to have bled out into the clouds. It reminded her of a song Lewis wrote, long ago, when she was a kid, but she had never bothered to learn all the words.

She made coffee and watched a man walk across the gas station, go to the hose and turn it on. He drank a while and then looked up, right at her, through the window, and she thought he looked like a little wind would pull him down the street, drag him away like a cold and cracking leaf and when he smiled at her she thought he might like it. He drank a little more, turned off the hose and came inside. He bought two cans of beer and said *thank you* with a voice so quiet, so rough, it sounded like someone had taken sandpaper to his windpipe.

Later, when it was warm, she went outside, stood in the sun, watched it dip down into that shimmer of red, never-ending desert.

The man was still there, sitting on a bench, asleep. He still had one can of beer left. She went and stood in his sun to wake him. He blinked up at her.

"You want to swap that beer for a cold one?" she asked.

He thought a minute, looked down the road, the same way she had been looking and stood up, his black eyes catching the sun, shining so bright she felt like maybe she should squint.

"That the fifty-four?" he asked.

"Uh?"

"Highway fifty-four."

"Yeah."

"Good." He nodded and followed her inside the store, went to the beer fridge and changed over his beer.

"You waiting on a ride or something?"

"No," he said. "Not anymore."

They walked back out into the sun together. His boots made a solid, comforting sound on the pavement and she wanted to reach over, brush away the dirt that was caught in that limp gray hair.

He nodded at the highway. "Know what's there?" he asked.

"Well, the Larson ranch, I guess."

"No, further."

"The ranch runs all the way into Texas."

He smiled and opened his beer, dusty thoughts waking him slowly and she thought of those snakes she saw sleeping in the sun, trying to bake themselves on the rocks behind the gas station, their heavy muscles rolling, swelling into themselves, until evening came and they began to disappear.

When she left work at three he was still there, on the bench, sweating under the sun. The wind danced in the road and she knew it would get cold that night, maybe drop to freezing, and she remembered the way Lewis smelled, for a little while, when he tried living with them and they had a wood stove he kept burning all through the night, even in June.

"You want a ride into town?" she asked.

He looked westward and frowned. "No. Thank you, but no. It's the wrong way."

"You going to Texas? Amarillo or something?"

"I got to get to Kansas. I got five weeks to get to Kansas."

"What's going on in Kansas in five weeks?"
The man smiled at the thought.

She woke late in the night and listened to her mother, listened to the soft talking, to the smooth sound of falling clothes and then that electrified silence and she got up, went outside, and walked behind the house where she could see that fire still burning, turning a corner of the desert sky into smoldering whisper of purple light. It looked warm, she thought, warmer than her bedroom had been and she wondered whose land it was on. She walked between the houses and saw Shawn standing on his porch, looking out at the night, drinking a beer in his undershirt. Not much over thirty degrees but he didn't look cold. He just looked lost. Blue shadows of televised light ran across his windows.

He heard her steps and blinked away his thoughts, smiled at her.

"Can't sleep?" she asked.

"Not tonight." He went to sit down on his steps and offered his beer bottle out to her. She shook her head. "You see your dad the other day?"

"Yeah."

"He still going strong?"

"I guess."

He looked across at Dusty's home, at the white pick-up truck parked in the driveway, taking up too much room.

"You see who it was?" Dusty asked.

"No."

She didn't believe him. The wind blew in that bone-cracking desert way, cold and clean, like it had been blowing forever and not come across anything but baked earth. Shawn pulled a wool shawl from the tub chair on his porch and held it out to her and when she put it over her she was surprised at how soft it was. She sat down next to him and they watched the sky. Someone laughed in the manager's office and she wondered if Aaron was laughing in his sleep again. When the wind blew right she could smell that fire out in the desert, smell the burning scrub and smoked air and she tried hard to see the flickering glow in the sky.

"Something's burning out there," she said.

"Larson land."

Later, not long after daybreak, Jo came out and stood on the porch, stretched -and saw them sitting on Shawn's steps. She grinned, gave them a girlish wave and almost bounced over to them. Dusty wondered how her mother could always look so young, always look so excited. When she sat down with them Dusty thought she may as well have been giggling.

"Whose truck is that?" Dusty asked.

"Wouldn't you like to know?"

"I keep sitting here, I will soon enough."

"Tim Larson."

"Where the hell did you meet a Larson?"

"At work," Jo said.

"A Larson went to the Golden Crown?" Dusty asked.

"Baby, everyone goes to the Golden Crown."

"You been seeing him long?"

"Just a little, here and there, for a few weeks now. He's pretty busy. He's got so much business always going on. You know he goes all the way to Dallas every single month. He says he wants to just move out there someday."

"He's not married?"

"Not yet." Jo winked at Dusty and came in close to her, hugged her a little for the warmth and she shivered.

Shawn looked at his beer again, looked at the inch of stale beer sitting in the bottom of the bottle and went back to staring out at the desert. "You better tell him his ranch is on fire."

He stood in the middle of the road, looking up highway fifty-four, his face tight, pinched against the dusty sun, sweat darkening the back of his shirt. Thin clouds, dark and streaked with a molten red, ran quickly across the sky and Dusty watched the man, wondered how long he would stand there, so still, waiting for that ride he already missed. She found an old *Western Horseman* magazine and started drawing an American paint horse, started at the eye like Lewis had shown her, but they kept coming out too angry, not sad enough like in the magazine.

The man came in and stood at the beer fridge for a while before mumbling, grabbing two cans of beer. He opened the first one as he walked to the counter. He counted out the bills and stopped, checked his pockets and pushed the second beer across the counter, away from him.

"Just the one."

"Sure."

"At least I'm not in Utah," he said.

"What's wrong with Utah?"

"3.2%."

"Uh?"

"The beer there. It's just 3.2%. It's damn near water."

He went back outside and sat on the bench. Watched the highway bake under the sun. He was slow drinking the beer.

She kept going with the American paint horse, trying to get it right and after a while, when the eyes were good and the mouth was wild, like the horse might break through the page, she stopped and went outside.

"It is damn quiet out here," the man said.

"Not much traffic goes this way."

"I keep hearing the land shake, like it's a cattle crossing or something but I think it's just in my head."

"Still need to get to Kansas?"

"In a little over four weeks."

"Might want to try getting out here in the early morning. Some truck routes take this way. Not many though."

"I'll keep it in mind."

"You got family there? Over in Kansas, I mean."

"No. No family. Just the wrong side of gone."
"Huh?"
"The wrong side of gone. 2200 pounds of wild muscle."
She looked at him, shook her head slowly. He sipped his beer and it made her thirsty.
"It's a bull. The wildest roughstock I've ever seen. They called her *the wrong side of gone*. Owners come up with fancy names for the bulls. I guess they think names like Simon or Walter and that won't become legend, won't bring up the fear from a man's stomach."
"You ride bulls?"
"I hang on for eight seconds. Call it what you will but that ain't riding."
Down the road, toward Texas, the air turned red, dust clouds hung low, hugging the highway and weak headlights glared out at them. Dusty frowned, stood back though she was far from the road. Heat beat down on them and then the white pickup truck whipped by, throwing the dusty air at them.
"Wonder how long it would take to walk it?" she asked.
"Eighty-six hours."
She looked up at him and thought he was too old to walk eighty-six hours and too old to be riding bulls.

She worked the night shift and come two o'clock she locked the pumps, turned out the lights, and drove home, watching silver clouds cross the highway, tumble through the cold, quiet night.
The living room lights were on, all the lights were on, and she took an apple juice box from the fridge and sat down in front of the television, waited for her mother. She watched John Wayne worry a while and got up, checked the house but Jo was gone, and later, when she turned out the lights and fell asleep in front of the television, the wind had picked up so that in her sleep she thought the desert sounds of scraping

and scratching in the night were her mother, home, walking around quietly, trying not to wake her.

When she woke up the television was off and the smell of smoke was strong enough that she worried that fire out in the desert might be spreading, heading over toward them. Thin veins of pink light played in the sky, and she laid back, listening for the sound of her mother, but all she heard was the nervous steps of a coyote outside, crossing the desert, lightly, wishing it was a ghost, and she knew her mother was still out, still gone. Spending time with a Larson. At the windows the pink light wilted in the sky like dying arrowweed and she walked outside, walked around the house and stood at the edge of the black desert. It was cold. Her breath showed, caught the wind and fell away into the night. She heard someone whistle and for a minute she thought it was Lewis, up from El Paso, hoping to see her, but he hadn't come north in nine years. She looked for the twitching light of the fire but it was gone.

The whistling grew and then she saw Shawn coming in from the desert, watching his feet, watching for snakes. She could smell the smoke and firewood on him. She knew the song he was whistling, some kind of Christmas song, but she couldn't place it. He walked by her, not more than ten feet away, but had no idea she was there. After he had gone she waited a minute, looked at the desert, tried to find that fire again. The wind blew at her and she thought it was too damn cold to be standing around and she went back into the house and sat in the dark, watching the light come to the windows, waited for her mother and after a while, once the sky was bright but still cold, still quiet and waking, she heard a woman singing that same Christmas song Shawn had been whistling and she went outside, stood on the porch and looked over at him, saw him sitting by himself, listening to the music, looking right at her. She waved and he grinned back.

He held out a coffee cup toward her and she went over. He gave her the coffee and went inside for a new one.

"You seen my mother?" she asked.

He nodded. "Yesterday. Maybe about noon. I guess it was Tim Larson that picked her up. Truck looked the same."

"Okay."

She could smell the fire on him still and wondered how close he had got to it.

"She'll be back soon," he said.

"I know."

The woman finished singing and he reached over, put the music on again.

"Why the hell you listening to Christmas music? It's July."

"Because it's good music."

"You know, I think that fire is gone. That one that was burning out on the Larson place."

"Yeah. I know. I put it out last night."

"Oh," she said. "Was it big?"

"Yeah."

It warmed up quickly and when the music stopped again Dusty looked over at Shawn and he had fallen asleep, his chin on his chest, and he had spilled coffee on his jacket. She saw the soot smudges on his hands and thought maybe he had been doing more than just putting out the fire.

That afternoon she called Lewis but he was out so she listened to his voice on the machine and then called back to listen again. She could almost smell the cigarettes. In the background she heard a soft, bouncing Mexican melody. Later, when she made hot dogs for supper, she made enough for Jo as well, then called the Golden Crown but they hadn't seen her since Monday night.

Before work she had a nap, listening to the wind.

She found him sleeping on the bench outside of Hondo's. He had changed his shirt and though this one didn't look much cleaner, it had a nametag, the patch sewn on. She didn't think he looked like a Gale. He had taken off his boots and was using them as a pillow. She left him sleeping and went inside. Carlos winked at her on his way out, his mind a thousand miles away, and she stood at the window and watched the highway change color with the signs. When it turned blue she thought of the ocean, wind swept and dusty, in a photograph her father had, of him and Jo, out on the coast before she was born.

Near midnight she saw him standing in the highway, looking toward Texas, toward Kansas and the wrong side of gone. He shuffled around out there, the cold snaking its way down from the mountains and across the desert and when he began pacing slowly, Dusty went to put on fresh coffee. The air began to growl and after a minute a motorcycle went by, going fast, going into town and Gale just stood there, watched it go and looked west again and shook his head. When he came inside the store smelled of coffee.

"Four weeks to get to Kansas," she said.
"Don't need to tell me."
"You want some coffee?"
"I'm out of money."
"It's free."
"Then hell yes, I want some coffee."

He looked over at the beer fridge and mumbled something. She made two coffees and he came over beside her, put in sugar. He looked at her a minute and she waited.

"Tell me something," he said. "This belt buckle is sterling silver. Worth maybe a hundred dollars, maybe sixty or so on a bad day. I give it to you, can I get some milk and one of those frozen burritos?"

"They're pretty bad."
"Sure I've had worse."

She looked at his belt buckle, at the dancing horses and the old gray dents. She tried to read it.

"You win that or something?" she asked.
"Yeah. I'd say ten years ago now. In Oregon."
"They have rodeos in Oregon?"
"They have rodeos everywhere."
"What about I just give you ten bucks?" she asked.
"Then I'll have something left for beer."

When she opened her wallet and took out the ten dollars he winced and looked away. He drank the coffee, looked through her *Western Horseman*, slowly, taking his time though she didn't think he was reading it, and a little before closing he got a burrito, a jug of milk and two cans of beer.

Jo woke her up. She sat beside her, in bed, and that wide, wide smile made Dusty want to laugh without knowing why. Her hair was still made up though it was nearly dawn and Dusty smelled the hairspray, smelled the bourbon, and something else, something musty.

"You're back."

"I was never gone, Sweetie. Not really. You know that."

"Anyone else here? Larson?"

"No. It's just you and me, baby."

She came in close for a hug. She buzzed with excitement, with memories and running, rambling plans, and Dusty hugged her back.

"Come have a beer with me," Jo said.

"It's almost morning."

"Well, it's still dark out so it's still nighttime."

They sat on the porch, in the quiet, in the dark. Jo couldn't hold still and the dim clatter of her bracelets was too loud. The lights were on in the manager's office and Dusty wondered if Aaron had fallen asleep at his desk again. The air was too still and she wondered where the wind had gone. The beer bottle was cold in her hands.

"You aren't drinking," Jo said.

"It's morning."

"Well then, give it here. This one needs company." She finished her first beer in a long swallow and smiled. "He's gonna take me to Dallas with him."

"Tim Larson?"

"Who else?"

"You're moving to Dallas?"

"No. Not moving, sweetie. When he goes next time, on one of those fancy work trips, he's gonna take me. Show me the sights. Wine me, dine me. He plays his cards right, the moving part will come along down the line. Honey, they got some real nice houses there, and he can afford them."

"Oh."

"You're gonna love it."

"I'm coming, am I?"

"What else you gonna do?"

"You know Shawn's gonna miss you."

"He's sweet but he's old and only has money the first of the month." She took a pull at the beer bottle and in the fading moonlight Dusty thought her mother looked young again, silly and at ease like she had been back when Lewis was around more. She grinned. "You know he flies first class? Drives to Santa Fe and then flies first class to Dallas."

Day came. Pale blue clouds started to glow, rolled out into the desert, and she could smell the fire again.

Shawn opened up his door, looked out at the sky, his face lit so that he looked like electricity was running through him, and he sat down in the tub chair and fell asleep. He frowned to his dreams.

Beside her, Jo sighed, happy.

When she came into work in the morning he was there again. Gale. Sleeping on the bench. A sad and syrup-colored sun clung to the edge of the land and the cold morning wind stung her cheeks, danced through the desert, whipped the Mexican feather grass until it sang. She stood over him.

He had his boots on this time, and an arm over one eye. He smelled like leather and wild grass and when she went to wake him she saw his belt was gone.

She left him sleeping and unlocked the pumps and looked up the road at a cow walking toward her, going slow. He gave her a wary look and angled away from the gas station, started trotting, its warm breath steaming at the nose. It was one of those Angus cows and she remembered Lewis telling her he always felt bad for them, that they always looked thirsty, wandering through New Mexico and Texas, dreaming about Wyoming and the green, green grass. It kept going, disappeared into the shadows of the highway, headed toward town, like somebody owed him money.

By mid-morning it was hot, bright, that shimmering heat played over the road, and when the beer truck came the driver was all sweat and soft words. She only heard half of what he said. He smiled, prodding, hoping, and she thought maybe he wanted a laugh. When she followed him outside to the truck Gale was gone.

After she stocked the beer fridge, she went back outside. The beer truck was gone and what with all the sun she couldn't see far. Sweat came quickly, built up along her back and pulled at her clothes and she went inside to draw but she was too restless and she looked through the gossip magazines instead, found a beautiful daytime actress that looked like Jo and cut out the picture to give her, tell her she was famous all along.

When Gale came in his shirt was open. Sweat darkened the arms of his shirt and his hair was damp, matted. She saw the thick scarring along his rib cage.

He went to the beer fridge and opened the door, stood there a few minutes, murmuring softly to himself. Then he buttoned his shirt and came back to the cash, put a beer on the counter.

"Two dollars, twelve," she said.

He counted out twelve dollars and fifty cents, and left before she could give him the money back.

She thought a minute and went outside, sat down next to him on the bench.

"How much did you get for it?" she asked.

He opened his beer, sipped off the foam. She thought it wouldn't stay cold for long.

"Fifty bucks," he said.

"Thought it was worth more."

"It is."

"Where'd you sell it?"

"Some place called the Golden Crown."

"My mother works there sometimes," she said. "I'm surprised you even got fifty for it at that place."

"Bastards didn't even throw in a beer." He squinted out at something in the desert, something far away and he smiled to himself. She looked but only saw baked red earth, feathergrass that looked as dry as dust, and that mean, simmering air. "Damn, it's hot out here."

"Only in the day."

"Good point. I wake up every morning with my feet so numb I think someone stole them."

She watched him drink his beer, sipping slowly, making it last.

He looked up the highway and frowned, "Eighty-six hours. Hell."

That night she ate alone, on the porch. The sun took a long time going down and the sky was swollen with that shocking gold of a dying light and when the light was gone, when the sky smoked and smoldered, dark with those hazy nighttime clouds, she could hear the desert owls wake and call out, worried and hungry, always hungry. She watched Shawn come out of the manager's office, cradling a six-pack of beer, moving fast with his head down like he was worried about being seen and he went into his place, slid the door shut and closed the curtains. Before going to sleep she checked her mother's room.

She found an American Bullrider magazine in town and brought it to work, thinking to show Gale. The bulls were big, she thought, but hard to draw. It was in the neck. They were strong, they kicked strong, but there was something in the neck that made her think they had given up a long time ago and she thought maybe there were just too many people, too many voices, so that all they wanted to do was walk away and keep walking until they found someplace quiet. There was a calendar and she saw two events in Kansas, in the first days of August, in Dodge City and Abilene. She put the magazine away and went out back, stood in the shade and saw a thick black snake sunning itself on a boulder.

Gale never showed and when she went home for the day she brought the magazine with her.

She made tomato soup for supper and sat outside, looked through the magazine again and when Shawn came out onto his porch to watch the sun go down she went over to join him.

"You think she'll hit jackpot?" Shawn asked.

"Who's this?"

"Jo. She went off to Vegas."

"She went to Vegas?"

"Didn't tell you?"

"No," she said. "She go with Tim Larson?"

He shook his head. "That didn't pan out. He was betrothed."

"Betrothed?"

"Set up to marry someone already. She went with Cam Higgins."

"Cam Higgins who I went to school with Cam Higgins?"

"He your age?"

"Couple years older."

"He grew up fast. Must be all that drilling. Good money in it though."

"I'll bet."

Nearby someone turned on a radio and serious guitar hummed an abandoned-sounding tune and she wondered if it was one of Lewis's songs, one of his old ones that had sold a little, that had played a little.

That night she walked out into the desert, walked all the way to the Larsons' land. She heard a lost calf whine but never saw it and when there was a sudden hush she was sure she had almost stepped on a rattlesnake.

She expected him at work again. Every time someone thin came in, or someone in a blue work shirt came in, she thought it was Gale, after a beer, after a ride, and when Carlos turned up early and told her she could head off, she took a beer from the back and sat outside on the bench, in the sun, and thought she knew what those snakes felt like.

When dusk came she drove out to the Golden Crown, parked across the street and watched the men drink, smoke, tell stories and lies, chase laughter. She had gone to school with a couple of them and knew they weren't old enough to drink, not yet, and when it came full dark she could see through the window to Mrs. Harrison serving a handful of old men who had been sitting there since she was a kid.

There was too much moon that night and she couldn't sleep. Cold air and silver light fell into her bedroom and it was late when she got up, went outside on to the porch and sat down. The sharp, wild smell of the desert filled the night and when she looked over at Shawn's he was outside, sitting in the shadows, watching her. He gave a tired wave.

That morning she woke up, alone, hearing horses run in her head.

The Luckiest Man in Town

Russell woke, his mouth dry and sour with fear. His back ached and his hands were stiff, raw, the blood swelling in his knuckles like he was young again, fighting again. A warm wind came from the window, pure and solitary-smelling in the way of pre-dawn hours. And he could smell the jasmine that Alice had planted in the garden, years ago, a proud talking piece for those dinner guests. She moaned softly, in her sleep, next to him, and when he looked down at her a small open-lipped smile played on her mouth. He touched his neck and winced. Sweat cooled on his skin.

Downstairs, in the dark, he made coffee, quietly, careful not to wake her. When the wind blew forcefully through the garden, rattling the iron patio furniture, he frowned. The front of the house was shut up, the wooden shutters closed and locked against the street, blocking the lamplight outside, trapping the air. He wanted to swim but knew she would hear the water in her sleep and wake.

Even with the glow of the streetlights it was very dark out, the sky low and black, thick as tar with the humidity, the moon wrapped up in heavy sheets of clouds. He could smell the river and, when he walked through the square and past a man sleeping on a bench, the rum and cherries of a long night of daiquiris. The man smiled in his sleep, happily and sweetly and Russell thought of how Alice smiled.

He sat outside, near the fountain, the river's wind playing at his back as it came over the levee, the smell of coffee and beignets making him hungry. Music played quietly inside, on the radio, and the waiters stood lazily side-by-side, watching a blonde woman's back. When she tied up her hair, he thought her neck was incredibly thin and the line of her lips was sharp and looked well bred. A waiter came and he ordered. She looked over at him when he spoke, looked right at him and sipped at a glass of milk.

"Think it's going to be hot today?" she asked. Her voice was very soft and lined with nerves, like she didn't want to speak.

"It's always going to be hot today." Russell smiled at her, still shaken, and looked down at his knuckles. They were smooth and clean and he rubbed them with his thumb.

"You work nights?"

"No. Just trouble sleeping."

"Nightmare?"

"Yeah."

A waiter came with coffee and sugared donuts, mumbled something under his breath about the woman looking fine. When Russell sipped his coffee and looked over at her, she was still watching him. The lamplight showed the hollow in her cheeks and he thought her smile would be a killer.

"They're good for you," she said. "Nightmares."

She left the café before dawn. When he watched her cross the street and walk through the square he was surprised to find she was tall. The waiters watched her as well, smiling, talking to each other. Wind blew down from the river and it was cold, crisp with frost from the north, but the sky was warming up already.

Russell looked up and saw the cook, in the back, watching him. He punched the air softly, twice, and smiled at Russell.

That evening he watched her from the kitchen, swimming laps. She was a fast swimmer and had sharp, energetic strokes that barely moved the water and he thought there was a lot of anger there. He remembered the first time he watched her swim, in the Gulf, not long after they had married and they drove over to Florida for three days. She had been skinny-armed and awkward.

When she stopped to rest she searched the windows of the house and he stood back into the kitchen, into the dark and her eyes moved on. The copper sky ran wetly over the water.

The doorbell rang and he frowned. Alice turned back into the pool and kept swimming. The bell rang again and he fixed a scotch and soda and listened to Wendell call out, letting himself in.

"I'm in the kitchen."

"It's dark in here. Why is the light off?"

"Bad headache."

"It looks like you're peeping on your wife." Wendell stood next to him and looked out the open door. He smiled at the sight of Alice swimming. "Is it true what they say about redheads?"

"Yeah."

"You didn't ask what they say?"

"It's true all the same."

They watched her get out of the pool, tie back her hair, her back arched like she knew she was being watched. Her skin looked hard, wet and bright with the fading sunlight behind her. Wendell sighed.

"Damn, Russell." Wendell shook his head and went to the dry bar. "You must be the luckiest man in town."

"You bet." He held out his glass and Wendell made them fresh drinks. "You ever eat at your own house?"

"Sure, but I do my drinking here."

The doorbell rang again and when Russell cursed, quietly, thinking for a minute he was alone again, Wendell laughed and went to the door.

He watched her throughout dinner, watched her laugh, watched her touch a thin man's hand encouragingly, getting him to talk more. He had seen the man before, he thought, talked to him even, told him an old schoolyard joke, but he didn't know who he was. When she cut her steak he noticed how tightly she held the knife, the joints of her fingers white with pressure and later, when he had gotten very drunk and fell silent, she looked at him with eyes so clear he wanted to think her simple.

That night he lay awake and watched a cold, pearl moonlight move over the bedroom window. It cast a pale shadow across the floor and over his wife. She looked young when she slept, he thought, sweet and young so a stranger wouldn't know she was made of iron. He fell asleep once, near dawn, when the wind that blew in from the bathroom window was warm and full of jasmine.

She had taken to watching him shave every morning, sitting in the window with the sunlight behind her so he couldn't see her face, only those long, lean legs coming from her robe. When he cut himself her legs tensed with excitement and he remembered his dreams. The blood ran down the edge of the razor and he washed it off quickly.

"No one uses a straight razor anymore," she said.

"I don't trust those little ones."

"You're bleeding."

"Only a little."

She smiled and came to him, pressed into him and kissed his neck. Her robe came open and her skin was firm and cold against his chest and she gave him the same smile she used when she told a man a dirty joke.

The next morning he left the house early, before she woke, and walked to the café. It was still dark, but the bars had closed and the sidewalks were being hosed down. The oak trees that lined the street were hulking shadows that moved slowly in the wind and he thought they seemed tired, worn out from worry. When he crossed the square, the wind blew at his neck, warm and wet against his skin, and he ran a thumb above his collar and looked at it, half expecting blood.

He crossed the street to the café, its lights burning brightly, showing the darkness of the heavy, swallowing sky. Louis Armstrong came from the radio and the waiters nodded absently to the music, watching the blonde sitting outside, near the back. He ordered as he walked in and sat outside, near the fountain. When the wind blew right he could smell expensive perfume and he was looking at her, wondering what she wore, when she turned to him.

"Not another nightmare?" she asked.

He nodded. He wanted to move closer, to sit with her. He watched her lips and they seemed to swell when she touched her tongue to her teeth. He wanted to see her smile.

"You have bad dreams too?" he asked.

"No. I like quiet streets and empty coffee shops." She turned so she faced him. When she crossed her legs her skirt came up to her thigh and she watched him, waited for his eyes to dart down, but he looked at his hands, spread out flat on his table. "What do you do?" she asked. "For work, I mean. With hands like that you must do something exciting."

"I sell advertising. My family owns the *Times*, I sell advertising there."

"That's not terribly exciting."

"No."

Across the street the first blue glow of morning light touched the square. The wind carried the smell of the river and Russell could hear, still down the street and out of sight, the rhythmic hooves of the skinny, twitching mules that pulled tourist buggies around town. Louis Armstrong still sang quietly from the radio, his voice young and the beat old, an early recording that Russell hadn't heard in some time.

"He sounded like Jelly Roll Morton back then," he said.

"Who did?"

"Louis Armstrong." He pointed to the radio, inside, on the counter. The cook was next to it, watching them, his chin buried in his elbows. When he smiled at them, at her, sleepily and slowly, like a cat stretching, she blushed and turned away. Small lines showed at the corner of her eyes and when she looked at Russell, looked hard at him and seemed to lose her breath for a minute, he thought the lines made her look very sad and very pretty.

"You have blood on your collar," she said.

He touched his neck with his thumb. His skin was rough and warm and he felt the torn flesh under his jaw. "Hell."

"Don't look so scared. It's just a nick." She smiled.

After work Russell walked home through the Quarter and when it started to rain he stopped in at an oyster bar that smelled of salted beer and air conditioning. Two women sat in the back, smiling at him, wriggling under their skin, their eyes dark and promising. He stood at the bar and watched the street. People ran past, screaming happily. The wind smelled like the muddy bottom of the Gulf.

"I remember you."

Russell looked up at the barman and blinked at him, trying to place him. He was big with dark, sweating skin and a dumb-looking, childish smile.

"I guess I've been here before," he said.

"Maybe. But I saw you fight. Over in Mississippi. You got old, man."

"Yeah."

"You still fight?"

"No. Like you said, I got old."

"You still look in fighting shape."

"I'm not. I get winded walking up the stairs to go to bed at night."

The barman smiled and looked around the room and when the rain picked up even stronger he raised his eyebrows, impressed. The French doors that lined the bar rattled in their hinges.

"Hey," Russell nodded at him. "When you saw me, did I win?"

"No."

"Hope you didn't lose any money."

"I won a little." He smiled at Russell and set a beer down, said it was on the house and walked to the back of the bar, wiping sweat from his brow with a cloth.

When he got home it was late and he was just drunk enough to be tired. The house was empty and locked up tight against the storm, the wood shutters bolted down, making it stale and airless. The radio was on, upstairs, in the bedroom and when he went up it was empty, dark and hot with the lack of air. He opened the bathroom window, stripped down to his shorts and went to bed. The pillows smelled of Alice, of her perfume and the particular woodland scent of her hair. He remembered when he met her, after spending time up north, in the Dakotas, the smell of her hair reminded him of the northwoods. He couldn't get enough of it.

She smiled when she cut him. A young, cute smile that turned up in the corners of her mouth, and she cut him again. He felt the warmth of his stomach opening, spilling, the blood running down to his legs. She pressed her body to him, holding him, her skin warm and her eyes wide and happy, shining clearly. He lay down, slowly, the dark and vibrant blood spreading, and she came down next to him and hushed him while she cut his throat.

He woke up, sweating, blood beating in his ears. He smelled rank, fearful and sour as a beaten cat. The light was on in the bathroom and he saw the shadows of Alice moving around, heard the water run, and heard the smooth sound of clothes coming off. He used to love that sound.

He heard them from the living room. She laughed a lot with Wendell. A good, strong woman's laugh and not the frivolous laughs Wendell was used to, that he got when he played at the Reunion. When they went quiet he knew Wendell was stuck, trying to think of something else, something good, and she was waiting. He heard footsteps and lay back on the sofa, put the newspaper on his chest and closed his eyes.

"Hey, old-timer." Wendell struck a match, lit a cigarette and Russell looked at him. Honey-colored light came from the windows and made Wendell look as dark as a pirate. He leaned on his hip like a charmed playboy. "Come on out before you get so old you mistake a bad memory for a clear conscience."

"That all you got?"

"I used up my best work on Al."

He followed Wendell to the kitchen and stayed standing in the door, away from Alice. She blew him a kiss, her eyes bright with alcohol and flirting, and cut quickly through potatoes. She was still in her swimsuit and water pooled on the floor. Her breasts swelled when she breathed and she smiled at Russell, shy and proud, and took a cigarette from an ashtray. When she stepped to him, quickly, with the knife out, he froze.

"Take over," she said. "I'm going to change."

Her hands were cold. She touched his cheek when he took the knife. He hadn't smelled cigarettes on her in years now. He held the knife tightly, down by his hip, away from her, and watched her walk down the hall.

Throughout dinner she watched him, coolly, chain-smoking, and when he looked at her, winked at her, she smiled studiously at him and he felt like prey. The wind blew and it smelled of steak and jasmine and the sky was a dry, deep lavender that looked like it might catch fire.

He woke before the nightmares came. There was a misting rain and it showed a running silver shadow outside the bedroom window and tapped steadily on the roof of the house. The bedroom smelled of Alice, of her perfume, of the gin on her breath, and he left quickly, without looking at her. He walked through the Quarter toward the river and when he heard the low, pulling sound of a late-night train going past, heading north, he walked to the tracks but the train was gone. The rain picked up. Warm, heavy drops caught the lamplight and made the streets glow with a rippling burning gold shine.

She was at the café, watching the street, frowning at the slow midnight traffic. Her mouth was tight-lipped, thoughtful looking and he remembered how good her smile had been. He wondered how she could sit so still with the Dixieland music from the radio, with the laughing rhythm of that clarinet. When he sat down the cook winked at him and went back to watching her. Russell could hear him humming at the radio, rolling dough in time.

She looked at him. "Couldn't sleep?"

"No."

"Can I sit with you?"

"Okay."

"Don't look so nervous." She smiled at him. She looked at him, watched him and licked her lips, softly. "What happened to your eye?"

He touched the scar tissue over his left eye.

"It's from a fight."

"In a bar or a ring?"

"Ring."

"I knew you did something exciting."

"More than ten years ago."

"And you still have the look."

The lights in the café shone brightly against the wet darkness outside and flickered like lantern light on her face. Her eyes were large, dark, and when she saw him smiling at her, slightly, thoughtfully, she looked away from him, nervous.

"Were you good?"

"When I was scared."

"Why'd you stop?"

"I passed my prime."

She laughed, loud and happy with the rain falling heavily behind her, swallowing the sounds quickly. She pushed back her hair. When the waiter came and set his coffee down Russell saw her cheeks had flushed. He rubbed his knuckles and looked down, listened to the radio.

"That the honest truth?" she asked.

"Sure."

"Ever kill a man?"

It had been a common question, long ago, after he stopped fighting, always asked with a flirtatious quiver of the body, with some excitement that made him gnaw into his back teeth. When he told her no, he hadn't, she bit her lip, trying to hide a small, uncertain frown. Behind her, on the street, the wind blew forcefully through the rain, shaking the oak trees. Two waiters that were standing at the edge of the marquee stepped back and brushed the damp from their aprons.

"Did you like it? Like fighting?"

"No."

"Oh?"

"I was too scared to like it."

"You lied to me, didn't you?"

"Yeah."

He wanted to see her smile again but couldn't think of anything to say.

It kept raining, hard, with the wind pushing deep into the streets. That night, after work he ate alone at the Reunion café, watching a group Wendell called the Tame Trio. They were too old to stand while they played, but mostly they talked about the rain, said a hurricane was coming, and smiled at a table of young women, forgetting their age. Russell ordered another vodka tonic and rubbed his knuckles. When the women left the trio played a thin, windy string of Duke Ellington numbers, stopping mid-song when the rain blew hard against the building and the doors flung open, something cracking.

The house was empty when he got home and he kept the lights off and took off his wet clothes, left them in the downstairs bathroom and made a drink. He switched on the radio and sat in the living room, in the dark, and listened to them talk about the hurricane. He made another drink, stronger this time, and thought the woman on the news sounded excited, breathless, and he thought people didn't know when to be afraid. It was only little, they said, but there was still time for it to grow.

When he woke up, sore from sleeping on the sofa, Alice was standing over him. Wind shook the house and he heard the rain run through the streets. He lay still until she left the room and he heard her go up the stairs. He unballed his fists and sat up, quietly, and looked at his hands, rubbed his knuckles and tried to steady his breathing. The rain came down hard, the sound overwhelming, and he wondered if the streets were flooding yet.

Later, when the moon had come out even with all the rain and the silver light cut through the storm shutters, Russell went upstairs and got into bed next to Alice. She mumbled in her sleep and he looked at her hair over her bare shoulders, falling into her face. The house shook under the wind and he wondered where the hurricane was, how close it was.

He didn't sleep that night. He lay, waiting, remembering the pleasure Alice had gotten when she kissed him, long ago, and she had bitten his lip hard enough to draw blood. He listened to her breathing, and when the light was bright enough at the window, looked at her smooth, baby-soft skin. She ran her arm over his chest, near his collar and he took her wrist. It was very small. Her fingers touched his neck.

"Russell, wake up. You're hurting me."

He held her wrist, tight, his eyes closed. He listened to the beating blood slow down in his ears.

"Russell," she said.

She tried to pull her arm away. He held the wrist, softer, and rolled onto her, kissed her forehead and tried to smile.

"Nightmare," he said.

When she kissed him back he smelled that old, bitter sweat of fear. The rain hit hard, beat steadily on the roof and even with the house shut up tight he felt the salt in the air, coming over from the Gulf.

A little before dawn the rain slowed and he ran through the streets and through the square. It was very dark and the wind was cold. The square was empty and in the lamplight the bare benches seemed small and somehow naked without the late-night drinkers and sleepers. He crossed the street and went into the café. A waiter nodded at him blankly and went back to watching the street. A stern voice came from the radio and Russell went to the order window, by the kitchen, looking inside the café at the empty tables. The cook was leaning on the counter near the window, next to the radio and turned it down when he saw Russell.

"Leave it on."

"She ain't here, man," the cook said.

"What?"

"She ain't here."

Russell looked at him and frowned. Outside, the oak trees shook heavily in the wind and dead leaves blew down the street, skipping sharply in the dark.

"You hear the news?" Russell asked. He nodded at the radio.

"Yeah."

"We going to get hit?"

"Made landfall a few hours ago, over in Mississippi. They always do that." He looked Russell up and down, quickly, settling on his hands cupped over each other on the counter, his thumb slowly rubbing his knuckle. "You want something?"

"A coffee. A big one."

The cook nodded, looked outside, at the empty tables going all the way back to the fountain. The lights buzzed quietly and he started to speak but turned back into the kitchen.

He sat down, at the back, near the fountain and listened to the radio, listened to the cook sing quietly to himself when the music came on. Day broke wetly, slow and dark like the city had sunk down to the bottom of the Gulf. Heavy purple clouds pressed in from the sky and the rain came and went, scattered and sudden and when he heard a train plowing slowly, out of sight, up near the river, he closed his eyes and smiled.

He watched Alice sleep. Her face was cold and hard, pale as old bone in the moonlight. He had opened the bedroom window and in her sleep she pulled the blanket up tight around her neck against the cool late-night air. Her arm lay over his pillow, the wrist smudged with bruising. Outside the wind blew dryly, the rain gone and the sky clear and pure. He sat back in the chair, in the dark beside the window, and looked at her wrist. When she stirred in her sleep, spoke softly so he couldn't hear, he froze, afraid he might wake her.

He touched his neck and thought of the dreams and remembered the last time he had been scared of someone.

All Gone Now

For a while he lived upstairs. In the early morning when the town slept so heavily, lost in that humid calm of the ending night, I could hear the soft scratching of him moving, waking, turning on those Sidney Bechet records so quietly I thought maybe I was still sleeping. But I knew better. Some days, some mornings, I would wake first and go stand by the window and look down the darkened street toward the river that I could always smell, always feel, rolling, pulling down into the Gulf, trying to take the town with it, and I would wait for him, wait for the music, wait for that wandering wail that always struck me as lonesome no matter how upbeat the tune. When he slept in I didn't like it. Those days were always off somehow. But they were few and far between and during the summer, when it was too hot to sleep more than a tangled hour or two and I woke to sit in the kitchen, under the air conditioner, reading the newspapers, I sometimes had the feeling that he was awake as well, waiting for some early hour he thought late enough for music. There wasn't much rain that summer and by August it was always too hot, too steamy, and the pills didn't help me anymore so I stayed awake, night in and night out, and I think he did too. Once or twice I could smell bacon frying and knew I was right and then came the smell of coffee and soon the sound of his mother's laughter when he woke her up and then the music. Always the music.

When I left for work that evening she was on the front step, smoking, watching the heavy oak trees wait for the wind. She took a deep pull and looked at me. I thought it was too hot to smoke, too hot to sit outside, or walk to work, and I thought those trees would be waiting for the wind until October. She smiled. It was a good smile, tight and a little frail but so was she. There was an equine lengthiness to her that made me half expect a nicker.

"You headed in to work?" she asked.

I nodded. It was dark already and her skin was pale and smooth under the light of the streetlamp. When she crossed her legs I looked away, chased my thoughts down the street.

"You work on Bourbon or something? One of the bars?"

"No," I said. "I work for the city."

"Heard you come in the other night. Must have been four in the morning."

"I'll try to be more quiet."

"You were quiet. I just wasn't sleeping."

"Too hot?"

"Too quiet." She smiled again and I got the feeling she wanted me to stay, to sit with her, talk with her. Sweat beaded lightly over her collarbone, over her shoulders.

"That your boy I hear sometimes? Playing those old jazz records?"

"Yeah. It is. Stewart." She smiled at me and started to roll another cigarette. Her fingers moved quickly, automatically, and when she packed in the tobacco, touching it softly, perfectly, I found myself wondering what it would be like on the receiving end of her touch. "Sometimes I wish he'd play something else. Maybe some Christmas carols. I love Christmas carols."

"I better go in to work now."

"Sure thing. I'll see you here and there." She picked up the *Times Picayune* and set it on her knees. I tried to see the front page.

"Anything interesting?" I asked.

She looked at the newspaper, took a deep drag and shook her head. "Missing children and budget cuts." She frowned and looked up at me. I thought her eyes might be blue, a thoughtful, deep, worried blue but really it was too dark to tell and when I smiled and walked away my mouth was so dry I had to swallow a few times to get it working again.

Even the Quarter was quiet that night, but still that small handful of drinkers I saw here and there were too much, too fast, too loud and I made my way to a darkened street and walked to work, put on the coffee machine and waited for the bodies.

When I got home in the early morning, before the river cooled the air, before the first drops of pale blue sunlight dripped into the sky, I sat down in the kitchen and read the newspaper. She had been right, the front page was full of budget cuts and missing children and I pushed the paper away, filled a mug with ice and water and waited to hear her boy start a record.

There was a shooting that weekend, in the Garden District, and the bodies came in early Sunday morning. There were three of them. One was too small. I could still smell gunpowder, still smell the rain and that warm, earthy smell of dying blood and I walked away quickly, down the corridor, hearing Claude's soothing voice echo over to me, telling me to take it easy, just breath and don't look at anything but the paperwork. When he sent me home early, I knew he had cutting to do.

I walked home through hot, heavy air and when I got to my building it looked too calm, unfettered, like a child left alone to play, so that I didn't want to disturb it and I walked on, went down to the river and to Harry's but they weren't open yet. I could see him, inside, slowly mopping the floor, his head swinging in time with silent music, getting ready for the Market traffic and I walked over to the park beside the Gazebo and sat on a bench, hidden from Harry's, from the Market and from most of the night by those dark, sweating palm trees. Across the street there was one early truck, the driver sitting at the back, under a streetlamp, reading the newspaper, waiting until he could unload. The air was clean and the slow smell of the river was overwhelming, brackish and muddy and very, very old and I remembered when I was young, long ago, when my father first moved us south and I spent my afternoons walking along the riverside, playing under the boardwalk and I saw a man and his daughter trying to tether a canoe to a piece of pipe. They stayed for two days and I watched them when I could and when they were finally gone I wondered what they were running away from.

Harry came outside and sat on the curb, alone, holding a gin and tonic that looked so fresh, so bright, I knew it must be lying and I remembered when I used to sit with him, drink with him, every morning, trying to decide if that was how to start or end a day. He finished the drink quickly and got up, went inside and I watched the moon grow dim and I sat on the bench until well past daybreak and tried not to think about the size of that body bag.

When I got home I sat in the kitchen and after a minute I heard the boy mumble something and I heard his mother laugh, light and delicate, like small waves at dusk lapping at a slow swimmer. The sun at the kitchen window was strong enough that even with the shades drawn the room was bright with a soft light and I closed my eyes and she laughed some more.

I saw her a few more times during the week, sitting out front, smoking those weedy looking cigarettes she rolled so fast, and each time I stopped to talk, tried to talk and it got so I'd spend time trying to think of things she might like to hear. I never came up with much. When I smelled the nicotine come the front windows, choking up that hot summer august air, I went outside.

"Where you off to, Billy?" she asked.

"Going to buy milk."

"You must drink a lot of milk."

"I do."

She smiled at me and played with the frayed edge of her denim shorts so that I found myself looking at those long, long legs.

"You know, all this talking, you never asked me my name."

"I heard your boy call you Jodi."

"And here I thought I still had some mystery."

"You do."

"Good." She patted the step next to her. The sun was still going down, hung low and bright in the scorched orange sky so that she squinted to look at me. She shook her head back, moving the hair away from her face and she reminded me of one of those strong racehorses my father used to run, full of nervous muscle under soft chestnut hair. "Sit with me for a bit."

"Okay."

"I hate smoking in the apartment. The smell never leaves and then when you want clean air you just can't get it."

I nodded. Music, something fast and brassy, came from the restaurant down the block and I could smell the happy smell of grilled hamburger, melted cheese and baked potatoes. Some nights I sat by my front window, in the dark, and watched the people walk down the block, heading into the Quarter, looking for fun. They always seemed like they would find it even if it wasn't there.

Jodi leaned into me a little. Pressed her leg on mine. The light through the trees began to darken so that when the wind blew through the leaves golden snakes of sunlight snapped through the air. I wondered what her breath would feel like on my neck.

"You cook a lot," she said.

"Yeah. I do."

"You ever work in restaurants?"

"I used to."

"I can smell it upstairs. Some days, I don't know what you're making but man, Stewart and I just go crazy, it smells so good."

I nodded and she grinned at me and I ran around in my mind trying to find something to say, but there was nothing there. Not anymore.

She laughed softly and took a drag of her cigarette. "If you're wondering what to say next, you should invite me to dinner, Billy."

"At my place?"

"Wherever you like."

I said okay, told her I'd think about what to make and we heard her boy, upstairs, start a Sidney Bechet record, the volume loud and I listened to that wandering open of "Blackstick" and I thought that even after all these years, after all that trying, there really wasn't much as wild as that anymore.

"I better get back upstairs," she said.

"Okay."

We stood up and she touched my hand, quickly, softly and I turned in toward my door and she laughed.

"You forgot about your milk," she said.

"I didn't really need any."

I didn't sleep that night. It was too hot, too quiet and I listened hard to hear them upstairs and later, well after the boy had gone to bed, I heard the soft moan of weight on the floorboards and that exciting sound of drink being poured out, being sipped at slowly and I went into the kitchen and made a glass of iced water and drank it at the table while I read the newspaper and tried to find the easy stories. Around four I heard some tourists hooting and I wondered why they had come out this way.

It was a quiet night at work, a good night, and Claude smiled sweetly to himself in that little boy way of his and thought I couldn't smell the vodka on his breath and afterward I walked home and made a bath so hot I thought I might not sweat for the rest of the summer and I stayed in the bath, adding hot water when it cooled. Pink daylight crawled across the windows and I waited for Stewart to wake up, to put on a record and I hoped for something soft.

He slept in that morning. The bath grew tiresome and when I got out the air was so humid, so saturated I thought soon I'd be able to grab it by the handful, and that warm water wouldn't stop licking my skin, beading up on me no matter how I toweled off and I went and stood in the kitchen, under the air conditioner in my shorts. By early afternoon the heat was crushing. When I was younger it used to rain every afternoon. The heat would grow until it was too big and something in the sky would break and I would run into the nearest restaurant or bar and wonder if the Gulf had turned itself upside down on the city. That didn't happen so much anymore. Now it rained in the spring, like we were up north or something.

My apartment couldn't take it, not even with the air on and the lights off and I went out for a walk, to find somewhere cool. The daylight somehow surprised me. I walked by Harry's and stopped a minute, watched the crowd at the oyster bar, their faces flush and eyes just starting to go glassy and I wondered what sweet things they were drinking before I moved on and saw Jude sitting at those chessboards, waiting for a game. I wondered why he never looked hot.

That night she came and knocked at my door. It was late and the heat had tapered off, wandered away with the sunset but there still wasn't any wind. I heard those easy sounds of him going to sleep a few hours earlier, heard the bathing, the murmur of those easy jokes he always made with her, the long still quiet of her reading and him sleeping. And then she knocked and when I opened the door she kissed me very softly but like she had been thinking about it for a long, long time. I stood there. I didn't really know what to do but she eased by me and walked into my kitchen and then stood there, waiting for me, laughing at me a little in that silent way.

Her skin was very soft and we were very quiet so that all I heard was the hum of the ceiling fan, working hard but still going slow, like the air was too damn thick even for those blades. When she fell asleep I noticed the childish smell of soap on her skin and the heavy frown of her brow and I didn't think she was sleeping very well.

A little after daybreak I heard him wake up, walk slowly around their apartment and after a minute he settled and I heard a record start up, heard that smooth wayward opening and I started to laugh.

She woke up and looked at me. She shook her head in question.

"I think he's teasing you," I said.

"Why?"

"That song he's playing, it's called *I Found a New Baby*."

"I gotta buy him some new records."

She went upstairs and I made Creole eggs and read the newspaper and after a while she came back and I made her some eggs as well.

"This isn't what I had in mind when I told you to invite me for dinner."

"I know."

She was a good eater and I watched her a minute then went back to the newspapers. I read them every day and usually wished I didn't.

"Christ," I said. "How may damn people kidnap children?"

She looked up at me. She thought a minute, then took the newspaper away from me and led me back to the bedroom.

If I dreamed at all that summer it was about beer, or gin, or crushed ice swimming in bourbon. The heat did that to me, and it got so hot I lay awake thinking maybe it wouldn't be so bad if a hurricane came through. Cool things down at least. Bring a little rain. Even on bad nights at work, when the closets were full, and Claude would shuffle around the corridor looking lost, trying to keep himself together and I hid behind the paperwork, hid behind the police, followed them outside to talk, take in some real air, I would still wander home and when sleep came, if at all, the first thing that came into my mind was beer so cold it hurt the teeth.

Some days I slept in, so that I heard Stewart and his music through that sweaty film of sleep, sunlight falling vague, filtered, somehow prying into my sleep, trying to wake me up and then I would hear Jodi laugh, hear the boy's fast running footsteps so that I wanted to join them but when I woke up it was too late and they were all gone.

One morning, I saw them together, walking down Decatur. She was tall, almost as tall as me, and lean so that she stuck out and when they got to the mules by the square Stewart stopped to talk to the animals. She watched him touch the mules softly, smile and talk while he held their faces, saying something funny so that he made himself laugh and it was nice to see how she looked at him. I was in the square, coming back from Dominico's and I was a little wired on coffee so that when I saw them, when I thought I had her eye, I waved frantically and knew I was grinning like a fool. But she didn't see me and she took Stewart's hand, crossed the street quickly and went up the block and disappeared by the parking lot at the river. I wondered how she could move so fast when it was so damn hot and I wondered would September be any better this year.

Sometimes when I tried to sleep, when I lay in bed and listened to the dried out hush of dying leaves crawl across each other, when the whole town seemed to sleep too easily, too quietly, I looked at my bedroom windows, looked at that pressing blackness and I was sure the night was watching me. If I slept it wouldn't see me. I'd be safe. But sleep was hard and so I got up and went into the kitchen, turned on the lamps, read the newspaper in the light, and waited for the sunlight to climb into the courtyard outside my window.

He played something different that morning. I don't know what it was. Some dancing trumpet that I thought might be early Armstrong or maybe King Oliver. I hadn't heard Oliver in a long while.

I listened to him walk around the apartment, walk around the kitchen above mine and I knew Jodi would still be sleeping. Later, when the music stopped I couldn't hear them anymore, couldn't hear footsteps or muffled voices or that quiet, falling laughter of hers. Daylight came in through the windows and I went back to bed for a few hours and listened to the hum of cars, to the call of ships, to the occasional running voice that was strung with some kind of electricity and I remembered going to Florida, to Panama City with my wife. Two of the fourteen weeks we spent together were on that burning white beach and at night, when those lights made the streets glow pink and blue and silver and all those colors that bring to mind the best tequila and the easiest smiles, my wife had that same electricity in her voice, in her eyes and when she looked away from me I knew she wouldn't be around for very long.

When I woke up it was still light out, still hot out, and I looked around my bedroom, wondering what had stirred to wake me. I listened hard but it was quiet and I looked at my chessboard and wondered if Jodi or Stewart knew how to play. The building moaned above me and I had the feeling someone was listening to me as well.

That night I went to work early and wished I hadn't. Claude was walking through the hallway and there was a small pale smear of blood on his scrubs. His dark skin was ashen and he looked right through me with eyes that only saw his vodka. When I saw them wheeling the gurneys through I turned and retched up water and bile. Claude shook his head.

I went to my desk and sat down. Another body went by and I turned away. Tried to breathe. Claude sat down across from me.

"You ever think you in the wrong line of work, Billy?"

"I don't mind a dead body," I said. "It's the kind of dead body."

He nodded. A paramedic looked in on us and frowned, then went back out into the hallway. I heard something thud and then someone laughed.

Claude reached for his water bottle but then set it on my desk.

"We get what the world spits out," he said. "Hell man, let's you and me quit. Go start a flower shop or some shit the tourists will like."

"They don't buy flowers. Can't take them home."

"Let's sell goddamned bullets. There's a real souvenir."

"Can't bring 'em on a plane."

"You ruin all my fun."

That night when we finished work Claude and I walked across the Quarter, over to the river and turned up toward the Irish Channel. We didn't talk and I left him in an all-night bar near Toledano that smelled of air conditioning and stale cigars and I walked home slowly, up alongside the river, going against the current. I had seen the river run inland once, after a hurricane that never made landfall.

I got home just after dawn and found a note pinned to my door that said *When's dinner? –J* and when I let myself into my apartment I heard him, already awake, listening to music, so softly I couldn't tell what it was and after I had a shower I got into bed and listened as he woke her up, speaking softly, talking on and on while she laughed very quietly.

There was a garage sale on next to the laundromat. I bought a cast iron frypan and a cassette tape of Bing Crosby's Christmas songs that I thought Jodi might like. They didn't have any Judy Garland. I fell asleep in the laundromat and when I woke the afternoon sun was low in the sky, casting those long, clawing shadows and I took my clothes and started for home.

A dark sedan was double-parked in front of the building. I knew the kind. They always had tinted windows and that dusty, stale look. I stopped across the street and watched it for a minute, wondering, thinking. Sometimes I saw those cars at work, outside, parked, trying to look forgotten. After a minute a thin man in a starched white shirt came out, looked up the block and got in the sedan and drove away. I went inside and unplugged my phone in case work tried to call me in.

That night Jodi came down for dinner, told me Stewart was upstairs, with a pizza, watching television. She kissed me and sat at the kitchen table, watched me cook.

"I got you some wine," I said.

"I don't need it."

She looked upward. We could hear the television, softly. He was laughing about something.

"He can come if you want," I said. "There's enough food."

"He's alright."

"I should meet him sometime."
"Not yet."
"Okay."

I made us some water with crushed ice and mint. I knew she was watching me and it made me nervous about how much I was sweating in that hot little kitchen, nervous about how I would smell of cumin and garlic, and when I looked down at her she had a wide, hungry grin. Her t-shirt was old and thin and clung to her so that I could see she had nothing underneath it and she took my hand, pulled me to her.

Later, when the night had grown old and quiet, laced with that fine silver light from the moon, we ate in the kitchen, with the light off and all the windows open. There was a warm breeze that cooled the sweat and carried the beautiful smell of those rotting banana trees that grew in the courtyard. It had been a while since I had seen the wind.

"This is good," she said. "What's it called?"
"Ropa Vieja."
"Mexican?"
"Cuban."
"You know your phone is unplugged?"
"I did that earlier."
"You that popular?"
"Someone came by the building. Some federal-looking type. I thought maybe work was trying to get me to go in on my day off."
"A federal-looking type? What's that?"
"He looked like an off-duty cop. Something like that. Sometimes they hang around if they need an autopsy done quickly. Lot of them owe my boss a favor."

She nodded and looked at her food. I wanted to turn the light on so I could see her better.

"Where did you learn to make such good Cuban food?" she asked.
"Florida."

When I woke up in the morning she was gone. I lay in bed and listened for them but all I heard was the wind scrapping around the courtyard and birds crying out for the rain. I had a shower and went down to Dominico's for coffee and later, when I passed Harry's I saw him, sitting outside, in the shade of the gazebo with a tall glass of gin and tonic, laughing to himself, his eyes glazed with something bitter. He didn't see me.

September came and so did the wind. It was heavy and slow, and it eased on up over the town most nights, full of salt and warmth, and later, not long before dawn, the night's air would cool off just enough that I could enjoy being awake; waiting, listening. Sometimes, at good times, I could still smell her on my sheets, on my skin, feel her breath down my neck though she wasn't there anymore. When things got bad I took a pill and then my sleep was swallowed up by those dreams that twisted, snake-like, waving and wandering away so that when dawn came and the music came, those dense laughing melodies of Bechet's clarinet would lead my dreams and my half sleeping medicated thoughts out over the Gulf so I'd be sure I was lost at sea.

I woke late that afternoon. It was quiet outside but I could smell her cigarettes and I went out to join her on the front steps. She smiled at me.

"You buy a lot less milk these days," she said.

"Yeah. I was up to three gallons a day for a minute."

"And I was smoking more than I wanted."

When I put my hand on her leg there was a hardness to her and after a minute I took my hand away. A tourist buggy went by and the driver grinned at me, pointed a finger at me and winked. I nodded back. Jodi rolled another cigarette and her quietness made me want a drink. The oak trees moved in the wind but I got the feeling they didn't like it. Somewhere birds were fighting.

She leaned her head on my shoulder.

I took my newspapers from the mailbox and we went inside. I started to make coffee, to open the papers and she took my hand, came close and kissed me.

Later, we lay in bed and I heard Stewart turn on a record, one of those happy clarinet tunes that France loved so much. The music danced in the night air, light and tight and I smiled over at Jodi and when I asked her if she wanted to stay, to have some dinner, she just stared up at the ceiling, her thoughts rolling on down some long, long highway. I tried to think of something that would make her laugh but didn't have any luck.

She took my hand, brought it to her mouth and bit it a little. "Hm? No. Not tonight. I can't."

That night I unplugged my phone and stayed home from work. I read the papers in the kitchen and when I got up to make another ice water I heard Stewart, upstairs, his voice running fast, desperate, chasing something. The wind had gone and the tight clinging grip of a humid night was settling into the air and I heard Jodi's soft voice murmur and then go quiet but he didn't stop, he kept going, kept talking, kept trying, until later, when I was in my bed, I heard her start to laugh a little, like she didn't want to.

I didn't sleep that night, I didn't try, and sometime before dawn I heard Stewart wake up, put on a Dinah Washington record I hadn't heard in some time and I listened to her laughing voice talk about television, listened to her tease about dials, and I heard the light tap-tapping of a child's dancing feet and finally a real laugh from Jodi.

I worked the day shift that week. It was never as hard but Claude wasn't there and the pathologist on duty was always too concerned. About everything. After work I ate at Dominico's and on the way home I stopped to watch Jude play chess against a college girl who tried to flirt with him. I don't think he noticed. I left before he saw me and walked up to the river and followed the levee into the Bywater. I looked in a few bars and wondered at how young the crowds were.

Later I sat in the kitchen and drank ice water, read the newspapers. Tourists walked by the front windows, their voices wired and dancing and I listened for Jodi or Stewart but I didn't hear them. Not that night.

In the morning I thought about leaving a note on her door but I couldn't come up with anything to say so I went into work. That night when I went to bed the streets were quiet and it was quite late when I heard someone moving around upstairs. I tried to follow the footsteps and thought that it would be something else to be able to make Jodi laugh like Stewart did, and later, I tried to sleep a little but when a ship's horn blew like a ghost's song in the night I knew I would be up until daylight.

That weekend I went shopping and when I came home there was a dusty sedan double-parked in front of my building and three police cruisers behind it. Their lights were flashing and hurt my eyes even in the daylight. Uniformed officers were standing in the building's doorway, away from the sun, still sweating, trying to breathe. The oak trees seemed to swallow the wind and all I felt was the damp, baked sunlight melting on my face.

I looked up at the officers from the bottom of the steps.

"I live just there," I said. "Am I good to go in?"

The same thin man I had seen before came out and looked at me. He pinched the bridge of his nose like his eyes hurt and nodded down at me.

"What you got there?"

"Groceries. Going to make my lady friend a gumbo."

"Lucky her." He waved me up and followed me into the building. We stood at my door. There were police walking around upstairs. Radios mumbled and I heard a man curse. I thought maybe it was hotter inside.

The man looked at me. "Say, you ever see the kid who lived upstairs?"

"Sure. Once or twice."

"That's it?"

I thought about it and nodded.

"How about the lady? The one with him."

"His mother? Well, yeah."

"That's not his mother."

"Really? I thought–"

He held up a finger and took a six by four photo from his shirt pocket. It was a mugshot of Jodi.

"Her, right?" he asked.

"Yeah. Jodi."

"Jodi?" He shook his head again. "Christ." Sweat ran from his hair and down his forehead and he wiped it away with an already damp shirt cuff. "Jesus goddamn Christ."

I looked at the mugshot. Her hair was lighter, shorter. It looked good. I think he wanted me to say something more so I smiled and tried to think of something.

"Look," he took a business card from his pocket. "She's probably in Texas by now. She won't be back. But on the crazy chance you see either of them again, will you give me a call? Okay?" I took the card and he gave my shoulder a pat. "Gumbo." He smiled at the thought of it and went back out into the sun and the heat. Somewhere down the block I heard a trombone start up.

I stood in front of my door and watched all the police, tried to catch what was said, what they wanted. One of the uniforms by the doorway looked at me in that dead, hungry way some cops have and I went into my apartment, into the kitchen, turned on the air conditioner and just stood there.

They stayed long into the night. Their footsteps were heavy upstairs, harsh and aimless and there was something needy to their voices when I heard them speak. I made water with crushed ice and mint and sat in the front room, near the windows, in the dark. Blue lights rolled in waves over the ceiling and someone lit a cigarette and the smoke came into my place. They left well after midnight and I lay in bed, my thoughts pounding, and knew that come morning there would be no wild, roaming clarinet, no music at all.

Nothing Shaking

I saw him through the window, sitting at the edge of the counter, smoking and fidgeting with his hat, his shoulders narrow but still strong. There was something very clean-looking about him. His hair was freshly cut, his white shirt thickly starched, and it pulled at me a little to see him sitting alone in the bony brightness of Dunn's. The Christmas lights had been put up and they flickered red and gold outside, on the street, caught in the snowfall and on the quiet, cold faces of the couples that walked by, heads down, cheeks scrubbed and pink. Inside the restaurant my father stubbed out his cigarette, pushed the ashtray away from him and looked at his watch. I went in, nervous to see him.

When I sat down he looked at me oddly, a sweet, lost smile at his mouth. He took a sip of water and smiled at me again. The restaurant still smelled of strong coffee and smoked meat.

"You look familiar," he said.

"I should hope so."

"That's not what I meant. Let's move to a booth." When he stood up I saw he was still taller than me. It was late and the blue of his beard was showing through and I remembered how rough it used to feel when he hugged me goodnight. He put on his hat and I followed him, looking at the eight-inch-high cheesecakes that lined the wall behind the counter. The waitress smiled at me like she knew me.

He watched me carefully a while, not saying anything, not drinking his coffee. His eyes were very black and seemed to burn as if aware of their own dark intimidation and I had trouble seeing my mother, with her clear, running-water blue eyes standing up to him, kicking him out on the street.

"Tell you what," I said. "For a newspaperman you sure write awful letters."

"Yeah," he nodded. "Guess I do."

I had received it on Monday, at work, and if it weren't for the *Tribune*'s letterhead I might have thought it a joke from one of the guys in the office. It was frustratingly brief: *Dear Kenneth, I would very much like to see you. I eat dinner at Dunn's every Friday night from 7.* He had signed his name and written "dad" beside it. I had reread the letter a dozen times, blinking rather stupidly, before throwing it away, but come Friday I knew I was going.

Behind me the door opened and I heard the wind and the snow, smelled the damp northern winter and the achingly cold river. My father was still watching me.

We ate quietly. He drank three, maybe four cups of coffee with his meal and when he took a sip he looked at me, nodding slightly as if confirming something to himself. After, he ordered a scotch and I had another coffee.

"You drinking again?" I asked.

"I never stopped."

"Oh, mom had said something. I guess it was years ago. Said you went into a clinic because of your drinking problem."

He shook his head. "I drank. She had the problem with it."

"So you never went to a clinic?"

"Not for drinking." He raised a finger to the waitress. "You've been eyeballing that cheesecake all night. Have a piece."

I felt like a boy again and wasn't at all sure if I liked it. He scratched his jaw and looked at me, the lines on his face long and deep and thin so you wouldn't see them from a small distance but when you did they looked like they had been there a thousand years.

"You like your job?" he asked.

"Well enough."

"I can understand that."

The cheesecake was incredible and he had a second scotch while I ate it. After we left Dunn's he walked with me to the subway. It was very cold and the snow melted into my shoes and the wind blew hard enough that it was all I could hear. Even with all the lights there was a darkness to the sky that night that swallowed up the streets. He shook my hand briskly and when he told me he was going to keep walking, to walk all the way home, I offered him taxi fare but he looked at me like I was crazy or stupid or both. Then he smiled.

"My uncle," he said. "You look like my uncle."

There is a photograph of my father, taken when we went to the coast, to a small resort town in Maine, and he is much younger, almost relaxed, sporting a slight, wind-blown pompadour. His arm is around my mother's waist but he's watching me, on the sand, his face flat and his eyes dark. Though my mother and I are in the photo he looks alone and he looks uneasy.

When I showed the photograph to my wife she said he was handsome but she wouldn't trust him. I stayed up that night, alone, on the sofa with a warm brandy, the pale, smoke-like snow blowing at the windows, and looked at the photograph and tried to see what she meant.

Later, after the snow had stopped and the cold, silver moon lit the apartment in a quiet way, I heard my wife, in the bedroom, moving, the sheets sounding harsh against each other and when I heard her light a cigarette I was reminded of my mother, when she used to wake late and unhappy and hard-thinking and smoke in bed until the alarm went off.

Seeing my father, thinking about him, made me restless and irritable at work. The girls at the teller all smelled too strongly of fine perfume and their vague flirting seemed to hide a nasty, long-term plan of divorce and second or third marriages. I remembered my mother's bitterness as she laughed at my father for working a job as dull as subediting at the *Tribune* while we went just a little hungry waiting for her alimony payment.

My tie was too tight and when, on Thursday morning after I hadn't slept well again, I loosened it and took off my shoes to work in my socks, I got reprimanded by the branch manager.

It snowed a lot that week and the river chill that runs through the streets stung colder, sharper than usual. The sky was low and heavy, dark even in the day and people walked hunched down against the wind, breath misting at cold, red lips. And with all the cold and all the snow the city became very quiet so that even in the busy hours after work there was the solitary feel of very late nights when the only sounds of life are the freighters.

On Friday evening I went to Dunn's again, hoping he'd be there. He was sitting at the counter again, smoking, looking dark and clean in the bright lights of the deli, nodding absently at the wall of meats and pickles and cakes as a big man next to him talked. The man nudged my father now and then, like a cue to laugh, and my father would smile a little, taking a long drag on his cigarette. A small, well-dressed woman joined them and I got the impression they worked together though we were quite a long way from the paper. When she talked, smiling, making the big man laugh, she looked at my father but he didn't seem to notice. He would nod, light a fresh cigarette and squint at the wall of deli goods as though he was seeing something else. He raised a finger at the waitress and she brought him a scotch.

I walked home in the snow. It was still quite windy, but there was a clean silence that I liked in the empty streets, and when I was almost home I passed Morton's and the chargrilled, burnt-salt smell of their steaks was too good to pass up and I went inside and ate dinner at the bar, alone. It was very dark in there and I looked around at the heavy redwood tables, at the solid booths with quietly eating men and women, and the over-the-hill waitress, and I thought maybe my father might like it.

A few days before Christmas my father sent me another letter at work, asking me to join him again at Dunn's. When I walked in the waitress was talking to him and he was laughing, quietly, softly, a familiar husky chuckle and his cheeks were cut through with dimples that had become deep scars. Frank Sinatra came from the radio behind the counter, singing soft Christmas carols, his voice too happy, too light. The waitress winked at me, said something to my father, and walked away.

"She still remembers you being a kid."

"We come here a lot?"

"Enough." He rubbed his face. The circles under his eyes were dark and his hair looked freshly cut again. "We used to come just the two of us. After your mom and I split. You remember?"

"A little. Before you went away?"

"Yeah." He nodded at the counter. "Before I went away."

"To Wyoming?"

He sat straight and looked at me, shaking his head a little. He took a cigarette from the package and tapped the tobacco tight. "No. Wyoming was before you were born."

"Mom said you were always trying to get back there."

On the radio Frank Sinatra started singing "Have Yourself a Merry Little Christmas".

"You know he had the words changed?" my father said. He pointed a strong finger at the radio. "Wanted the song to be more damned jolly."

We moved to a booth and ate, my father watching me as he washed his food down with several cups of coffee. When he smiled, handsome enough that I thought the girls at the newspaper must find him dashing, there was still that particular sense of loss in his face, around his mouth, that I had seen in the photograph of our family on holiday. I asked him if he had plans for Christmas and he waved a finger in the air for a scotch.

"Sure, I have plans," he said.

"Well, I thought maybe you'd want to have dinner with us, with my wife and me."

"Your wife." He nodded. "I forget you got married. I forget you're old enough to." He drank half his scotch down in one swallow and looked at the waitress. She nodded to him. "She a good cook? Your wife, I mean."

"She's okay. Good enough."

He finished his drink as a fresh one came and a little later, when he had his third, I noticed he didn't change like most people do. He didn't loosen up, his eyes didn't brighten with expectation. He sipped slowly, watching me with burning black eyes that made me feel like wounded prey, and, when he spoke, softly, measured, his voice was unchanged.

That night I had a drink with him, in Dunn's, at the counter, listening to Christmas carols, to Frank Sinatra then Judy Garland and my father smoked and smiled.

I saw my father several times over the next few months. Always at Dunn's, on Friday's from seven, sitting at the counter, alone. When he saw me he would smile, sweet and lost, but still tall enough, hard enough, and with eyes black enough that they seemed threatening.

At the end of March my wife and I went away for Easter and spent a few days in the mountains. It snowed heavily but it was a wet snow that ached in the bones and we spent the time inside, listening to music, drinking warm brandy.

On Monday we took the morning train home and when we went through the station, the holiday crowds smiling and laughing around us, I saw my father asleep on a bench. My wife hadn't met him yet and I was about to stop and introduce them when I saw that he was oddly filthy and, on coming closer, smelled like a vagrant who had been given a bottle of sour wine.

I turned us away and steered my wife out of the train station and into the wet, windy streets.

When I was a boy, and had gone some time without seeing my father, I asked my mother to tell me about him. She said he was dull. He rarely drank a real drink, preferring Pepsi-Cola, and lapsed into mean-eyed silences for no good reason, silences that might last days, she said. I knew he worked and didn't see how that could be true.

Three weeks after I had seen my father at the train station he wrote me at work, asking me to dinner. I called him at the *Tribune* and when he came on the line, saying his name in a calm, rasping voice that reminded me of sawdust, I told him I was taking him out to Morton's, that I knew his birthday was in May and wouldn't take no for an answer.

"That'd be fine," he said, and hung up.

That night my wife found me up late again, drinking the last of the brandy and looking through old photographs. She took the photograph I was looking at, one of only four or five of my father, sitting on the front steps of our old house, reading the newspaper. She shook her head.

"He looks like he wants something from you, from everyone. Be careful."

I told her about Morton's.

"That place is expensive."

"I know. It'll just be the once."

She gave me a kiss, looked at me like I was still a simple-minded child, and went back to bed.

The night I met him at Morton's, standing out front in the wind, smoking, his face dark and red under the lights from the sign, I was nervous. I'm not sure why. He smiled when he saw me, his face splitting with wrinkles. It was cold for May and the wind ran hard between the buildings, still slightly crisp with a lingering winter, but he stood straight and didn't lean into the wind. I could smell the strong, salty river and, from the restaurant, the hot coals and thick steaks.

It was odd seeing him in the dim elegance of Morton's. He smoked, careful and steady, watching the restaurant, wincing slightly when bursts of laughter came from other tables. We ate quietly and I thought of those mean-eyed silences my mother had talked about. Once in a while he shot out a question, and halfway through the meal he called the waiter over and ordered two single malt scotches, expensive ones, and kept them coming.

When I asked him why I didn't see more of him when I was growing up he blinked at me like I should know the answer, then seemed to change his mind about something.

"Some men aren't given much say in those situations," he said.

I nodded. I didn't ask about him often when I was young, but the times I did my mother told me he was away, out of town. "Ever make it back to Wyoming?" I asked. "After the divorce?"

"No. Almost went, once, quite a few years ago."

"Still miss it?"

"Yes."

"Why?"

A woman laughed at a nearby table, loud and longing, and my father looked at her, dark-eyed and silent. "The air is good out there."

He left before dessert, saying he had an early start with the paper and when I finished my coffee and went to pay I was told he had already settled the check. I walked home, the streetlights bright over the damp sidewalks, the wind still going strong, and bet myself that my father had walked back to Dunn's for a coffee, at the counter, alone.

The letter looked like an overdue tax notice and I didn't open it until late at night, when I went to the kitchen for a glass of milk and saw it was from Saint Mark's Hospital. He was in a recovery ward and the doctor who wrote the letter strongly advised that I pay my father a visit. There was no mention of what had happened or why he was there. I sat down at the kitchen table, the spring moonlight very bright and the air very fresh through the windows, and read the letter again. I didn't sleep that night, I didn't try, and before dawn, when the waking city sounds of delivery trucks and doormen arriving for work carried softly through the streets, my wife came and sat with me. She read the letter and looked at me but didn't say anything. After a while she held my hand, then put on coffee. I thought she was very beautiful in that gentle, golden morning light.

I went to Saint Mark's early. When I was directed to the psychiatric ward on the third floor I thought my father must have had a nervous breakdown. I found him asleep, alone in a cold, sterile ward, his face and hair dark, rough-looking like a wood splinter against the ivory walls and bedsheets. The rope burns around his neck were quite noticeable. He looked cold and his lips were cracked from the dry, regulated air. I took a blanket from the neighboring bed and put it on him then sat down.

After a while I noticed a doctor was standing back, watching me, too young and too nervous to be looking after people.

"You look a lot like him."

"I was always told I take after my mother."

He shrugged.

"What happened?"

"He tried to hang himself. Superintendent found him. He must have been there all night, dying in fact, but I guess he got lucky. Strong bones."

"He doesn't look very lucky lying there."

"All the same, he is."

"Shall I take him home?"

"Not for a few days," he said. "We need to watch them for a few days. They'll often try again."

"Jesus Christ."

The doctor raised an eyebrow at me and excused himself.

That afternoon he woke, coughing and smiling like a boy who had been caught skipping school. When he scratched his chin, watching me carefully, I heard the hard rasp of his beard against his fingers. The hospital was by the river and a ship's horn blew. My father's eyes burned, slowly, blackly, and when a nurse came clucking over he looked at her and she stopped, stuttered something and turned away, laughing quiet and nervous. I kept looking at his neck. The skin was raw and looked like badly tooled saddle work and it made me think of when my father lived in Wyoming, before I was born.

"How's it look?" he asked. He touched his neck, near the rope burns.

"Bad."

"I thought it might." He lit a cigarette, nodded at me and looked out the window. It was a fine afternoon and the spring air was warm, the sky almost painfully bright blue and I heard a radio from somewhere in the building, playing a soft, singing jazz. My father coughed at his cigarette and sat up to put it out. His hands were rough, hard and strong with thick slate-white nails and I thought they didn't look like the hands of a newspaperman.

That night I watched him fall asleep then left, quietly, and took the subway home. When I came up onto the street I stood on the corner and it was a clean, clear night so I could see my building down the street, see the new doorman even, and I turned the other way. There was a stiff wind coming up from the river that made me hungry and I walked to Morton's and sat at the bar, drinking scotch I couldn't afford. I ordered a steak but when it came the moist grilled meat reminded me of my father's neck and I pushed the plate away and ordered another drink.

The next day I left work late, after dark, and walked to Dunn's. The streets were crowded even though it was raining and people walked past, quickly, heads down and faces gray and grim in the wet light from the store windows. Dunn's looked warm and even outside in the street I could smell strong coffee and smoked meat and when I walked in and shook off my raincoat I half expected to see my father sitting at the counter, smoking, listening to his own quiet thoughts. In a booth near the front sat a large man and small, pretty woman, both dressed in tired-looking, gray suits, and when the man saw me he looked at me twice, his face and eyes pinched in thought. The woman said something that made him laugh and forget me and I ordered a pair of sandwiches and coffees to go.

At the hospital my father was awake, reading the newspaper and smoking slowly, an ashtray on his lap. He hadn't had a shave in three days and the stubble looked out of place on him, made him look quite old and weathered. When he saw the takeout bag from Dunn's he laughed, silently, his body shaking and his grin wide and he folded the newspaper and set it on the bedside table. His neck was still dark, bruised and raw but in the clean yellow light from the lamp his face, or rather his eyes, looked healthy and even happy. Rain struck the windowpane hard and fast and the hospital felt warm but damp and I didn't think there was one open window in the entire building.

"The lady at Dunn's asked about you," I said.

"What lady?"

"Waitress."

"What'd you tell her?"

"Told her you had the flu."

"She believe you?"

"No. Couldn't see why not though."

"I go there when I got the flu."

"Oh." I added cream and sugar to my coffee. "Anyone need to be told? Work or anything?"

"What? You gonna tell them?"

"Sure. If need be."

"No," he said. "No one needs to be told."

It rained hard that night. My father fell asleep not long after we ate, his face flat and tired, his wide, serious mouth lined and dry. I took the empty coffee cup from his hand and he woke up, grabbed my wrist hard and looked at me so that for a minute I thought he might hit me, but he smiled slightly and fell back to sleep. His breathing was rasped and I wondered if his throat was rough and scarred on the inside as well. He didn't let go of my wrist and even in sleep his grip was hard and wiry. Newsprint and tobacco stained his fingertips, but even so he still looked clean and he still looked strong.

I got home very late that night and my wife was still awake, in the living room, drinking red wine and reading a magazine. Her feet were tucked under her and she looked like she had been taught to sit so ladylike as a girl and never grew out of it. When she kissed me her breath was sour with the wine and when she didn't speak I knew she must be on her third or fourth glass. The windows were wide open and rain and wild, fresh wind came into the apartment so that it seemed the building shook. I sat down in the armchair across from my wife and watched her read, the air tense and hostile and silent and I wished I looked more like my father.

When I went back to visit my father, I was told he had checked himself out that morning.
"I thought he had to stay for a few days."
"Well, we can't really force them now. Can we?"
"I thought you could. I thought you were."
I went to Dunn's three nights in a row and sat at the counter, drinking coffee, alone, the waitress watching me, smiling at me in a way that made me feel like a boy again, and I waited for my father. The evenings were warm now and when I walked home the air was soft, smelled clean and salty and the streets were bright with the silver moonlight. I slept badly. I kept my wife awake though she didn't say anything about it, and at work I was tired, my eyes sore and my mouth sour with fatigue. On Friday morning I called the *Tribune* and asked for my father but was told he was on leave. I watched my wife make coffee. Her robe was very thin and when she moved it pressed into her body, drifted over her bare skin.
"Just go to his apartment," she said.
"I don't know where he lives."
"You know his name." She took the phone book down from a shelf and put it on the table. She smiled at me, tired, bored, her lips and cheeks oddly tight-looking.

The superintendent let me in, nervously, his face folded up in fear of finding a hanging man again. He stood back, in the hallway and out of sight, smoking a cigarette, waiting. Weak morning sunlight came through the windows and lit the apartment, showed the fine dust in the air, struck brightly at the wood floors. The smell of old newspaper and ink hung in the air and the apartment was very clean, the floors deeply waxed. I opened a window as a train went past, heading west, its whistle blasting happily.

I could smell coffee and there was an unopened bottle of single malt on the table, but the apartment was empty and had the cold, ghostly feeling of not seeing much company.

That summer my wife left me. It was in August when the city becomes unbearably hot and still, when the wind dries up and the river seems to stop moving. She had been smoking more and more, and even with the windows open the cigarette smoke hung in the air, moving heavily and everything smelled of ash. When she smoked she watched me, quietly and with a great and feminine hostility that made me smile at her and try to win kisses I didn't want. I saw it coming weeks away and didn't care. Many nights, when she opened a bottle of wine, her back to me and her dark hair shining with the need of a wash, I left the apartment and went out to Dunn's.

She moved away at the end of the month and I found a small apartment near Front Street that was very sunny in the mornings. At work beautiful girls smiled sadly at me but kept a good distance, and in the evening I walked until I was hungry enough to go to Dunn's where I sat at the counter, alone, drinking strong coffee and listening to Frank Sinatra on the radio and I thought about my father and I thought about Wyoming.

Clear Midnight

That winter it was bad and he often woke a little before midnight with his teeth aching and he would dress quickly and walk through the snow for an hour or so and later, when he came home, he saw the lights burning softly at her window. She didn't seem to sleep much. Sometimes he stopped in the hallway and listened at her door but there was little to hear. Once he heard the squeak of a cork but there weren't any voices and he liked the thought of her having a late-night drink, alone, while the building slept.

He saw her several times in the elevator and always nodded and looked away, quickly, afraid to hold her eye. She was young and kept odd hours but there was something about her that made him think she was recently divorced and happy with it. When they got off at the same floor she smiled that wonderful, wary smile pretty women develop and he wanted to introduce himself, wanted to hear her speak, maybe even hear her laugh, but instead he gave his own wary smile and walked quickly to his apartment.

There was a snowstorm after Christmas. A bad one. It took the city two days to clear his street and when he woke at night he looked out the window, looked at the hushed, buried streets and went out walking anyway, his feet falling, sinking deep down into the snow. He walked all the way to Front Street, down to Dusty's but they were closed and he stood in the snow a while, thinking hard in that cold air. Ghostly blue light from the café's sign drifted over the snow, danced with the small wind that played in the air.

When he got home it was late and her lights were out. He looked up at the building and a man came and stood next to him.

"You got a cigarette?" The man asked.

"No."

"Hell."

"I quit last year."

"Take it up again."

Hugo smelled the nicotine coming off the stranger, and the raw, wind-blown scent of worn-out leather that made him think of being a boy, of waiting for his father to come home again.

They looked at each other.

"Maybe you could spare a few coins?"

"Yes," Hugo said. He held up two large silver coins, grinned, and when he put them in the stranger's hand he coughed, like his father had taught him. The man held up a five-dollar bill and blinked at it.

"Good trick." He put the money in his pocket.

Hugo looked at the man. He was enormous. His beard and hair were thick and matted and he nodded up at the darkened building.

"She pretty?" The man asked.

"Who?"

"Whoever lives in those windows you were looking at."

"In her way," he said. The wind blew. A long, thin wind that stung Hugo's cheek and he looked at the man. "Okay."

"Okay."

Hugo nodded to himself and walked up the steps, kicked snow from his boots, shook the snow from his hair but it had melted already. He wanted a scotch but it was too cold.

Behind him he heard feet falling into snow but when he turned around the man was still standing there, looking up at the building.

"There's a laundry room in the basement," Hugo said.

"Oh yeah?"

"You can stay there if you want."

He took the man down in the elevator and let him into the laundry room. It was warm in there.

"Look. A lot of old people live here. I don't want any of them to come in to do their washing and have a stroke or something when they find you. You'll scare the hell out of them. You're too big. Over there, that door, it leads to the alley out back. Just let yourself out in the morning."

"You got it."

"What's your name?"

"Eugene."

"Good name. It was my father's name."

"He's dead?"

"Yes."

"Recently?"

"No. Ages ago. I was in my thirties."

"Still got your mother?"

"Oh yeah. Death can't kill her."

It got a laugh. A small one.

When he came home from work she was stepping out her door and he nodded to her, taxes and sour voices running through his head so that he knew his smile was off, weak and wandering and nothing she would want to look at, and when he got into his apartment he went to the window and watched her out in the street, holding her coat closed at the neck. She hailed a taxi with a sharp hand. The wind pulled playfully at her hair.

He was home the next two nights and not long after dark he saw her down on the street again, dashing into taxis, looking like she was running late. At least the city had cleared the snow. She would get wherever it was quickly. He ate his dinner at the card table so he could watch the street, watch the snow drift off the piles the snowplows made, watch the cars thin out until there was something aimless and longing to the occasional headlights that lit up the streets. He had a drink and went to bed early but he woke a little before midnight, opened a window for the cold air and dressed. In the hallway he stood a minute at her door.

Outside he crossed the street, turned south, toward Dusty's, and he saw her windows were lit. After a minute someone moved, rolled their shadow over the ceiling and he remembered waiting for his father to come home one night, watching from his bedroom window as the moon grew larger until he noticed his father's small figure standing in the street, smoking a cigarette, watching the house.

Up on the eighth floor another light came on and someone stood at the window so Hugo walked away, quickly. He didn't know anyone on the eighth floor.

It was cold in Dusty's and he ordered a slice of apple pie and cheddar cheese and when Edna brought it to him he grinned up at her.

"I was feeling off, but you turned me on."

"You've used that one before."

"It's good enough to use twice."

"If you say so." She sat down and lit a cigarette. "I'm freezing. Even with the heat on, I'm freezing." She looked him over. "You walk down here? Subway doesn't run this late."

"I walked. I like it."

"You're turning into your dad."

"Next up, my vanishing pie act."

"His jokes were better."

"Sim sala bim."

It was almost dawn when he left. The wind was sharp enough to draw blood and the streets were empty, quiet, so that those thoughts were loud in his head, and they tapped heavily at his brow and he wondered if that was what his father had felt like, if that was why his father would stand down the block smoking, watching his house when he had already been away so long.

His cheeks were numb when he got home and he liked it. The sky was a pale, northern blue and the clouds were dark, almost black like they were still holding on to the night, trying to pull it back over the city and when he walked into his apartment it was freezing and he remembered he had left all the windows open. He made coffee with his coat on and drank it by the window, looking down at the street and in the dim, dubious light of daybreak he saw someone across the street, standing in a doorway, smoking a cigarette, watching the street and watching his building with the same nervous posture his father had. Hugo finished his coffee and realized that the man was almost as big as the doorway and he thought it must be Eugene, back, hoping for another night in the laundry room. He wondered what brand of cigarettes Eugene smoked.

She smiled at him and held the elevator door. She looked pretty, subtle and pretty like a woman who is meeting her father for dinner, but she wasn't going out. They rode up together and Hugo smelled her perfume, that warm, expensive smell of a damp overcoat and he was sure she had cold cream on as well and he wondered if that was to keep her skin soft against the windburn. He grinned at her and wanted to say something, better still do a trick for her, but too many ran through his mind until he thought of a few of the more morbid ones his father had come up with at the end and when he thought of these he found himself laughing in a quiet, private way that he worried she might find inappropriate. But she didn't hear him, didn't notice him and she seemed surprised when the elevator stopped at their floor and he waited for her to leave.

"Oh. Sorry," she said. "I don't know where I was."

She stepped out and Hugo gave her a soft smile and saw her eyes were red and held that sparkling clarity of held back tears. He followed behind her and when she came to her door she turned back, looked at him in a way so he knew she was nervous as hell.

"You have a good night," he said.

"Likewise."

He went quickly to his door, went into his apartment and locked the door behind him. He hoped she heard the bolt snap.

That night he didn't bother with sleep. Thoughts rattled and his jaws ached and when he thought of the woman down the hall he worried in a different way so that finally he got out his father's old notebooks and a deck of cards and practiced a few of the harder tricks, something to impress people at the store. His hands shook and he couldn't move the cards right, couldn't slide them or hide them and he wondered how his father had always been able to. Cold air crawled slowly up his back and he looked around, quickly, nervously, but he was still alone. Later, he made coffee and drank it by the window, half expecting to see his father out there, in the street, alone, watching something in his mind.

Wind fell heavily through the streets, rattled the windows, and the snow tore through the night, danced through the air like a wicked horse, struggled to catch the sad and pale light of a hidden moon. Later, well past midnight, Hugo dressed and went out, stopped in the hallway, outside her door and listened, heard the tender, teasing sound of ice falling into itself inside a cocktail glass and he wondered what she drank. Vodka maybe. He couldn't imagine her drinking that scotch he liked.

In the morning, when he left for work, he stopped in front of her door. She was laughing. It was a good laugh, full, deep and real and beautiful without trying to be. He touched the doorknob.

After work he walked through the rush-hour streets, the sidewalks filled with red-cheeked shoppers and weary office workers. Tired school children followed their parents, happily lost, their thoughts a thousand miles away, somewhere free of those parents they followed so blindly, until he turned down toward Front Street, toward Dusty's where the streets were a little quieter and the people a little shabbier, a little colder. Edna brought him meatloaf and he remembered when his father started bringing him to the city, where they ate, and, when Hugo was old enough, where they drank. It didn't take much to get his father going. Two old-fashioneds and he was flushed, talking too fast, thinking of new towns, new shows and new faces and wondering how to give them more and give them better.

While he ate he watched Edna take down the Christmas lights and he thought it was too soon, that they should stay up until March, brighten things up a little. Make the world a little warmer.

He went to Babylon after dinner, treated himself to a Balvenie with two ice cubes and watched them melt while he listened to the piano run riot, chasing those awkward sounds and he thought that the smooth-looking man sitting up on the stage was trying to come up with something different but throwing beauty out the window. Different will only get you so far, he thought, and never far enough. He finished his drink in a swallow and walked out, back into the night and he walked fast and when he got to his building he looked up, saw her windows were dark and he kept going, kept walking, trying to chase something that was burning in the back of his mind. Edna was right; he was turning into his father. It started to snow heavily so that he couldn't see more than thirty feet ahead and the whole city was a quiet, humming blur of gliding headlights that got caught in the bustle of swiftly twisting snow.

It was late when he got back to his building and he looked up, tried to see her windows, tried to see her, but with the weather he couldn't make out anything. Behind him, someone lit a cigarette, coughed softly and then there was the smell of nicotine.

"Remember me?"

"Eugene," Hugo said.

"That's right." Eugene offered Hugo a cigarette.

"I don't smoke anymore."

"Of course," he said. "You quit last year. What brings you home so late?"

"I went for a walk."

"In this?"

"I have trouble sleeping."

"That so?"

"Well, I can sleep alright. I mean I can go to sleep just fine. Early even. It's the staying asleep that's hard. I get three hours, four if I'm lucky and then I'm up, wondering what's going on. Just once I'd like to clear midnight."

"I get that."

"But you sleep in doorways."

"Not every night."

Hugo tried to smile up at him. Up on his floor he could make out the warm golden glow at a window. He counted along from the corner of the building.

"I'm leaving lights on," he said. "I don't usually do that."

"That you on the fourth floor?"

"I think so." He watched the windows. The light seemed to move, slowly, from window to window, wandering like a lost ghost until it went out and the two of them stood in the street looking at the dark building.

"Guess you're gonna have to buy new bulbs."

"My father used to do this trick, late at night, when we were alone in the house and it was dark. If he went to the bathroom or kitchen or something, he'd unscrew the bulb from the lamp and walk with it, still burning, through the house, using it like some witch's lantern. He thought it was funny but it scared the hell out of me."

"But he's gone now, right?"

"He's gone now."

"I used to know a trick."

"What kind?" Hugo asked.

"An escape trick."

"What did you escape from?"

"Everything, I guess."

"You want to stay the night in the building again?"

"Downstairs?"

"That's right."

"Yeah. Okay. That's probably a good idea."

Hugo waited while Eugene finished his cigarette. The slow, almost wary way he smoked made Hugo think of his father, of the way he watched his family in the days before he was taken away, and Hugo wondered if Eugene knew how to escape from handcuffs too.

Come Saturday he took the day off and went to the museum. It was warm inside and the calm sound of whispered voices echoed off all the marble and he found the mammoth his father used to sit in front of for hours, thinking, sketching out his ideas, his acts. Hugo watched the old animal and wondered what his father saw. After an hour he found he was frowning and chasing those pulling voices in his mind and he got up, left the museum, and walked down the block to the Clover Grill.

She sat at a booth, alone, looking at him as though she expected him. When he walked over her eyes grew wide and he wished he had gone somewhere else.

"Hello," he said.

"You live in my building."

"That's right."

"Do the pipes rattle all winter long?"

"Yes. It's the heating system. Old buildings." He shrugged and looked at her hands. They were well manicured but had that raw look of hard work. He remembered a trick his father did and thought they might not be her hands. The thought made him smile.

"It's cold in my apartment. No matter what I do. I think the wind must come in from somewhere. And someone on our floor leaves his windows open. I can smell the cold air in the hallway."

"Yeah." He thought a minute.

"Are you meeting someone for lunch?" she asked.

"No. I was just going to get some coffee."

"Have some fries with me. They always bring too much. But I hope you like vinegar."

Hugo sat down and nodded.

"You always dress so dapper," she said. "Tell me what you do. Unless it's something boring."

"I sell magic tricks," he said. "I have a store."

"Oh! Well. I can't decide, now. Sales is boring, but magic…" She gave him a teasing look through half-closed eyes. Her lashes were thick and reminded him of a horse. An incredibly pretty horse. "Can you show me a trick?"

"I'm not very good."

"Just a little one."

"You look cold," he said.

"I am."

A waitress brought the French fries and he asked for a coffee while she doused them in vinegar. The waitress winked at him and walked away.

He reached inside his coat and brought out a wool scarf. It was neatly folded.

"That's mine!" she squealed.

"Thank god."

She laughed again and he wondered at what that laugh had got her over the years, wondered how carefully she worked it at, made it just lost enough, just naïve enough, made it just right for a man to try to protect her. She took her scarf and put it on, giving him a look.

"I'm Mary, by the way."

"Hugo."

"It's good to meet you. Properly. We see each other enough."

She ate slowly, holding the fries delicately, as though they were rich and rare chocolates, and she watched him with a small smile tugging at her lips. When the front door opened she shivered before the wind got to them.

"Oh, this cold is something else. And when have you ever seen so much snow?"

"Last winter?"

She laughed again and he wanted to get another one out of her. Keep them coming until he had heard them all. He tried to remember some of the lines his father used, the good ones, the ones that worked on the people that didn't want to be there. When she took a deep breath, sitting up suddenly, he wondered at how soft her lips looked.

"My time is up," she said. "I'm afraid I have to meet a friend for lunch. Someone who doesn't ever eat. And it's all the way across town so I have to catch a cab now."

"Okay."

"Let me give you something for the fries. You barely touched them."

"It's okay. I'll settle it with my coffee."

She smiled and walked quickly out of the diner. She moved lightly and he watched her, out in the street, her small, rough hand in the air, squinting against the wind and the cold silver sun, and he wondered why she looked frightened.

The faint, hugging smell of her perfume stayed with him, stayed on him, for most of the day and later, when he was alone in his apartment he didn't want to cook anything for dinner, fearing that the great bashful scent of whatever she wore would be overpowered. He made a drink and sat by the window and watched as the street darkened, watched as the world and the night grew quiet and dark and the buildings around him switched off their lights so that the snow on the streets took on an eerie and sad silver shine from the moonlight and when he saw Mary step out of a taxi, her overcoat gone and her hair tied back in a sharp ponytail, he turned off the lamp beside him and watched from his darkened room as she stepped through the snow, her legs far too thin, her face far too tight that he thought she must wake with screaming teeth as well. When her breath showed in the air he thought it would be cold and smell too sweetly of old gin.

He slept for an hour and woke suddenly. It was quiet and his apartment was too warm but he left the windows closed, dressed and left. The elevator smelled of cigarettes and when he got to the lobby he stopped and looked at the front door, looked at the way it was propped open with the new telephone books. Wind blew snowdrift into the foyer, wind that smelled of an empty world, and he buttoned his coat, started to leave, but instead he went back to the elevator and down to the basement. He left the light off and walked toward the laundry room. The door was open several inches and he could hear the man snoring. Hugo thought for a minute and went back upstairs, back out into the streets and walked down to Dusty's. He hoped Edna had some blueberry pie. He felt like blueberry.

It was one of those nights that bit lovingly at the skin; cold glass kisses of wind, of snow and dancing moonlight came at Hugo as he walked home from work. Carter had come into the shop before closing and stayed a while, talking, remembering, smiling for something that wasn't there anymore and Hugo locked the front door, turned out the lights at the window case and sat in the back of the shop with Carter and let him talk. He listened to the stories about his father and laughed quietly where they had changed a little until Carter's blue and bleary eyes softened and Hugo called him a cab and they stood outside in the snow, waiting, the golden lamplight humming above them.

The front door was open again and the lobby smelled of perfume, of cocktails and soap and freshly scrubbed skin. He waited for the elevator, heard the bright laughter falling down the shaft and when the doors opened a pair of handsome men and a well-made woman looked at him and suddenly laughed again like he had finally come up with a good punchline. The woman had very green eyes.

When he passed her apartment the door was open. She was on the sofa, a tall drink in her hand, her fingers delicately dancing over the glass while a man stood over her, talked to her, talked softly with a deep, hard voice. Hugo smiled at her but when she looked at him she just kept on looking. He walked away quickly, nervously and let himself into his apartment and made a whiskey. Outside, snow fell against the black sky and he opened a window, looked down at the doorway across the street but it was too dark and there was too much snow to see all the way. He made another drink and thought about going out to Babylon for a Balvenie but he didn't want to hear the music, not like that.

He fell asleep briefly. He woke before midnight and went to the window. The snow had picked up and the wind dashed it across the sky and he put coffee on and ran coins while he waited for it to brew. He was getting slower, he thought. He kept dropping the coins. He shut the window and turned on his heating and when the pipes started beating he remembered Mary, sitting in her apartment, looking like a little girl getting in trouble. She had been wearing a dress that was too thin for the weather.

After the coffee he put on his coat and went out. He stopped at her door and listened, hard, wondered if the soft movement from inside was just the wind. He put his hand on the door and it was warm.

Outside there was too much snow, too much wind and he couldn't see, could barely walk and he crossed the street and looked up. Her lights were on, dimly. He stood there a minute, thought about Eugene, and went back across the street, back into his building and up to his place.

In the morning he left for work early. The superintendent and a cop were standing in front of Mary's door, laughing quietly about something. They stopped when they saw him but the super still smiled.

"Hey, Hugo," he said.

"Hi, Barry." Hugo looked at the door, saw the splintered wood around the lock. "What happened?"

"Someone pried the girl's door open," Barry said. "You hear anything last night."

"Just the wind."

"Yeah. Some storm. Still bad out there."

"She okay? Mary, I mean."

"She wasn't home. Freyberg in four-oh-six saw it this morning. Woke me up."

"Oh." Hugo looked at the door and thought a minute. The cop rubbed his hands like he was cold even though the heating had kicked in overnight.

"I heard the storm is going to last at least two more days," Barry said. "Do snowstorms have category levels, like hurricanes?"

The cop shrugged and looked around, trying, Hugo thought, to see where the smell of coffee was coming from.

He took the elevator to the basement, switched on the lights, listened to the hum of the building. It smelled of steam and detergent and, faintly, cigarettes. Eugene wasn't down there. Nobody was. Hugo stood in the laundry room a minute and thought about Eugene until his thoughts wandered on to his father. He remembered the last routine he watched his father work on, remembered that odd laughing, almost proud, smile on his face because he knew he had come up with something great.

When he left the building he closed the door, made sure the lock caught, and looked across the street, looked into the doorways, but there was nobody there. It was too damn cold, he thought.

It took a long time to walk to work and the snow came down hard all day.

When he walked to Dusty's the snow had stopped falling but he thought the air might turn to ice. The streets were empty though it was still early enough for dinner, for excitement, for cocktails with new people, for the soft hand-touching he always saw when he went to Babylon. He tried to think of a joke, an old one, a good one, something that Edna might not have heard in a while, not since his father was around. He turned onto Front Street. When he got to Dusty's he saw Edna standing at the window, watching the empty streets, drinking coffee that still steamed. He waved to her but she didn't see him.

She brought him coffee and waited while he looked up and down the menu. He kept reading it, turning it over, waiting for her to say something.

"You know you're gonna get the meatloaf," she said.
"Hrm."
"Take your time." She looked at him, waiting.
"I used to think I was indecisive, but now I'm not so sure."
"Oh god."
"How do you make antifreeze?"
"Steal her jacket. Come on Hugo, you're gonna have to do better than that."
"I'll keep trying."
"I know."

After dinner he wanted to hear music but it was too cold to walk that far even for him and the taxi would be too expensive. He walked to the corner of Lexington and bought a bottle of single malt, then turned for home. When he got to his building he looked up at her windows but they were dark, most of the building was dark, and going up in the elevator he thought he could smell her perfume.

He made a drink and noticed he bought the same brand his father often got when things were good, when he wasn't worried, and he lay down on the sofa and fell asleep after his second scotch.

He woke a little past midnight, dreamtime voices echoing in his mind, in his apartment, and he went to the door and listened. The voices still murmured. He opened the door but the hallway was empty and he walked down to Mary's and stood outside, listening. He touched the door, listened hard, but it was quiet, the whole night was quiet and he went back to his living room and stood at the window.

There was an ambulance parked down there. Two paramedics were talking to Barry, all of them next to a stretcher with the biggest body he had ever seen lying on it. He stared for a minute, then sat down on the edge of the sofa. He suddenly felt like sleeping. Down below, Barry kept nodding his head in that prodding way he had. Hugo stood up and went quickly to the elevator but by the time he got to the lobby the ambulance was gone. He saw Barry standing outside, looking down the street but he didn't want to talk to him, not now.

That night he slept on the sofa, waking often throughout the night, listening to the wind cry down from the north. A little before dawn he made coffee and sat at the card table and tried to deal cards from the middle of the deck, but he couldn't get it right.

On Thursday he worked late, kept the shop open longer, half hoping Carter would come by, have a drink, tell those stories. A young father came in with a little girl and he showed them the linking rings and the girl's black eyes danced, happy, excited and he saw the way her father kept squeezing her hand softly. By ten Carter didn't show so Hugo closed up and walked home, happy with the quiet starlight that flashed over the snow.

Lights were on in her apartment and, when he went upstairs, her front door was open but there was a young man inside painting the whole place white. The apartment was empty and looked very cold and later, when he woke not long before midnight, he opened his windows for the fresh air and saw a man, across the street, smoking in a doorway, thin, nervous shoulders turned against the wind in that familiar way, and he wondered if Edna had any apple pie.

Mount to the Sky

When she told him to hurry, that they were late already, he thought of all that foundation the ladies wore, thought of how it would get onto his jacket, onto his collar as they came in for those light, expensive-smelling kisses. He listened to her heels on the floor upstairs and took his drink onto the back porch. It was almost dark and deep purples slipped over the sky, and he could hear them again, next door, yelling. He liked the sound of the girl's voice when she yelled.

He watched her come out of her house, quiet now, and stand in the driveway. She was very thin, he thought, very small, too small for such a voice. She looked around and kicked out at a tricycle and he took a step backward, into the porch, into the dark.

He heard Lori come up behind him.

"She's younger than your scotch, Allan."

He nodded and finished his drink.

"You ready to go?" she asked.

"Gin."

"What?"

"I was drinking gin."

"Good for you. Let's go. Any later and they'll think I had to drag you."

"You do."

"Hurry, hurry."
"You look great."
"As good as your young friend?"
"Better."

When they left the girl was sitting at the curb, smoking a cigarette. She looked cold, Allan thought, cold but happy with it and when she took a deep drag, watching the sky, he tried to remember that Greek god with little wings at his feet.

Allan watched the girl rake leaves. It was early and the sky was dim, gentle, an easy November blue that seemed to say it would always be so quiet and he smiled, still waking, still dreaming, and when she looked up at him he didn't register. He came back to himself and saw she was frowning at him and he felt old. He blinked out a smile and went into the kitchen to start the coffee. From the counter he could still see her, through the window, raking, looking happy with the work and with herself.

Lori came down the stairs, already talking. He didn't know if it was to him.

"I'm going to walk to work," he said.

"Walk? But it's cold."

"I like the cold."

"They say it will snow this week."

"I hope so. When we were young there was always snow by November."

"You must have had a different childhood."

"Coffee?" he asked. He kissed her, gave her a mug. She still smelled of whiskey sours and someone else's cigar.

"I need a hot bath," she said. "Scalding."

He looked out the window, looked next door. She was still there. "Think she'll do our lawn?"

"Who?"

"The girl."

"Chloe. Her name is Chloe. And I'm not game to ask her. Yesterday I thought she was going to murder her father."

"That's not her father."

"Still, it was nice her mother got a break from it." She laughed, sipped her coffee and looked over the kitchen, over the living room behind him. He wondered how long after he left the house before she would pour herself a drink.

When he left for work the girl was sitting on the curb again and when he nodded at her she frowned weakly, with nothing behind it and he knew she wanted to smile. He stopped.

"How's Rudy?" he asked.

She studied him a minute. She wasn't good looking yet, he thought.

"You know my father?"

"A little. We had a drink together, once or twice, before the divorce. That seems like so long ago now."

"It was."

"He still spend all his time on the road?"

"They don't tour so much in the winter. He'll be spending the next two months here in town."

"Does he still smell like horse shit? I used to love that smell."

"Me too," she said. She smiled at him and he thought maybe he was wrong; maybe she was good looking. He wanted to touch her cheek but she was too old for that. Or too young. He wasn't sure anymore. "He'll be here soon if you want to wait."

"I can't. Tell him I said hello."

When the snow came he was awake, downstairs, a prowler in his own house. It fell fast and full, bright against the windows, and he went outside and stood in the cold. Down the block the light from the streetlamp was dim, muted by all the snow, and when he coughed the sound rang out. He looked at the house next door and wondered if the girl still had her room upstairs, at the back. She had been a quiet baby and he remembered that lost and laughing look her father always had when he played with her, rolled her around on his belly in the garden. And he remembered her father's quiet face when he had to go on the road, down to Texas, over to Wyoming; he remembered watching the two of them sit on the curb, watching the sun go down, when she was about three, not long before he was told not to come back, never to come back. He wore a brown felt Stetson, the hatband a braid of white horse's hair, and he put it on the girl to shield her from the sun.

They had been to a party, another one, and in the morning his head hurt. Voices, old conversation, and missed jokes, ran through his mind, repeating themselves and when he heard the glass break he thought it was imagined. He looked out the kitchen window and waited but they were quiet. The young trees outside were bare and looked a wonderful and twisted black in the morning light. He set bacon in a pan and heard the girl's mother, heard her frayed voice all ready to break and he wondered who had thrown what.

The girl came out and sat down on the porch steps. Her mother came out and stood behind her, stood over her, her shoulders wide in her long black coat, wide enough and black enough that Allan thought she looked like an owl watching a mouse.

"I'm leaving now," her mother said.

"I'm waiting for my father."

"Don't hold your breath."

When she got in the car, when she looked at her daughter, Allan wondered if she might drive straight into the porch.

After she left, Allan watched the girl, ate the bacon straight from the frying pan and wondered why Harris had spent the night smiling so shyly at Lori. Harris was not a shy man.

A roughed-up Buick pulled up at the curb and he heard a wild guitar from the radio. Rudy got out and stretched, grinning, but his face was too hollow and his eyes too gray to ever really look happy. He cupped the girl's head with a big hand then they got in, drove away, the music rambling after them. Allan shook his head. It was too damned early for bluegrass.

The lead-up to Christmas excited Allan and in the morning he put the outdoor lights up, over the front porch. It was snowing again, lightly, and when she came out of the house, very quietly, he almost didn't hear her. He plugged in the lights and switched them on. They were red and silver, a little cold without the green, he thought, but clean looking. He looked over at the girl, sitting down at the curb, smoking a cigarette. The nicotine smelled good in the cold air.

He walked to the curb.

"Aren't you a little young to be smoking?" he asked.

"A little," she said. "You want one?"

"I stopped a few years ago."

"I know. You always smoked in the backyard. I could smell them from my room. I missed it when you stopped."

"You liked the smell?"

"Not really. Not then." She looked over her shoulder, at his house, at the lights. "I like those lights."

"Me too."

She looked so small sitting in the curb, like a swift wind might pick her up, thrown her about with the snowdrift, and he sat down next to her, looked down the street at the dark, sleeping homes. There used to be more Christmas lights out, he thought, a long time ago.

"I heard you last night," she said. "Heard that music you were listening to."

"Nat King Cole."

"It was nice."

"I didn't think anyone could hear me."

"Not anyone sleeping. I was awake."

"I hope I didn't bother you."

"You didn't," she said. "You're always up late. Or early. Either way, you're always up."

"Guess I'm worried I'll miss something."

She looked at him like she didn't believe him.

He heard his front door open behind them, heard the silence of Lori watching him with the girl. She would think of something smart to say, something sharp that he couldn't come back from, and she would save it.

Later, when he left for work, she was still out there, still on the curb, lost in dusty, faraway thoughts.

It caught up with him and he fell asleep early, downstairs, by the Christmas tree. When he woke it was dark and Lori was still out. The lights from the tree lit the living room and for a minute he remembered the way Lori used to laugh. It was a delicate laugh, like fine, woven crystal that danced away and invited him to follow.

He heard Chloe, next door, growling, and he sat up and looked at the tree, at the lights and thought it all looked a little bare without gifts, without wrapping. He listened to her yell, listened to her mother, tried to make out the words. He heard something about Rudy and went to the kitchen for a scotch and he drank it at the window, watching their house, waiting for something to move at the windows but saw nothing but snowdrift, whipping at the air, lost between their homes. He fixed another drink, a tall one, full of ice and when he poured the scotch he noticed the bottle was close to empty and he wondered who Lori had over.

Chloe's mother got louder, yelled out *No no no* so loud Allan stepped back. Out the window the snow picked up and he moved to the front porch, into the cold night, let the easy sound of the wind drown the yelling. The snowfall was coming on faster, heavier and he thought come morning the streets would need to be plowed. The door slammed and he saw Chloe walk out of the house, walk down to the curb and sit down, wrapped in a ranch blanket, and after a minute he heard her crying. A soft and quiet cry and he remembered the panting whimper of a coyote he had hit with his car the last summer.

The falling snow caught a car's headlights. A door snapped shut and he heard Lori's familiar step; small, precise heels hitting the pavement, a happily determined rhythm and he saw her come up their pathway, her head turned, watching Chloe. She stopped for a second, her long dark hair caught in the wind and he could just make out the line of her lips, the soft open mouth. She nodded slightly to herself and walked on, left the girl alone.

She jumped a little when she saw him standing in the dark, on the porch.

"Keeping an eye on her?"

"Keeping an eye on you." When he kissed her she smelled of gardenias. "You smell terrific."

"I should hope so. You bought the perfume." She started inside the house. "Are you staying out here? It's freezing."

"I'm coming."

"Is she crying?"

"I think so."

"Fighting again?"

"Yes."

"Did you hear it?"

"Not the words," he said. "I heard them mention Rudy."

"Rudy? The cowboy?"

"Yes."

"God, is he back again?"

"I guess so."

"I hope I don't run into him. There's always something so damned depressing about him. Gets me down every time."

Allan followed her into the kitchen. She took down a glass, made herself a drink and then another one while he watched her. She had gotten thinner all of a sudden, he thought. Her collarbone seemed like it might snap under a hard kiss and he walked up to her and ran a finger down her neck, along her collar.

"Christ. Your hands are like ice." She moved his hand away, kissed him easily on the cheek and smiled that dinner-party smile. "I'm going to shower. Give me a minute and come join me?"

When she walked upstairs he heard something whip and bang outside, down the back, and he walked to the back door. The girl was out there, in her backyard, smoking a cigarette, her head down as she watched something in her hands. She moved quickly, lightly, her hand snapping at the air and he saw the lasso cross her yard and catch the handlebars of a child's bike. She pulled it down hard. When she took a long pull on her cigarette, her face was hard, was serious and hollow.

He left the party early, without saying goodbye to the Davenports, to the Scotts, to Lori even. He couldn't remember when he had last seen Lori. Early, before they brought out the champagne, before the singing, talking in whiskey-soaked whispers to Heather. Laughter still rang in his ears, the greasy smell of makeup and starched hair lingered and he walked quickly through the snow, the heavy swollen clouds low in the sky, pushing in on him, stealing the air. His mouth was thick with gin and his mind wandered, quickly, aimlessly, through homes and seasons and he remembered a Christmas from years ago, when he started staying awake nights. He remembered the mean and dashing look in Lori's dark eyes that didn't fade when he kissed her, and he remembered staying downstairs, watching Rudy and Chloe walk down the road, the two of them carrying a Christmas tree as the snow billowed like wild white birds around them. She was small then, and serious. She held the back of the tree and when they came up the driveway to the house they both looked at him like they thought he was not real.

He saw the Buick up ahead, parked, the engine running. Cobwebs of silver moonlight ran through the sky and Allan stopped, watched the car and wished he still smoked. He walked over and knocked on the car window. Music played very quietly inside the car.

Rudy stepped out and walked around the car to Allan. His coat was old, worn out, and didn't look warm enough for the winter and when he held out his hardened hand Allan smelled the horses that Rudy spent all his time with.

"Jesus, Rudy, you must be cold."

"It's not so bad. Not with the heater going."

They shook hands. Rudy looked older, thinner, and in the dark evening Allan could not make out his eyes but felt something lonesome and wandering in them. He grinned at Allan and shivered into himself.

"You just stalking your old house?"

"I guess I thought they might still be awake," Rudy said. "Well, I thought Chloe might still be awake."

"She usually is about now."

"Still bad at sleeping?"

"Still bad at sleeping."

"Me too," Rudy said. "It's not so bad if I'm here, in town. I can drive out and take a look at the old house, see who's awake, watch you sneak around your living room. On the road, though, it ain't as much fun."

"Still riding?"

"Oh yeah. Mostly do roping these days, but still riding." He looked up at the darkened house. Snow wandered slowly over his face, over the street and across the sky and when the moonlight broke through the clouds Allan saw how old Rudy had become. "How she doing anyway?" Rudy asked. He nodded at the house and looked at Allan, hard.

"I guess she's okay. Doesn't seem to like Wallace very much."

"Smart girl."

"You teaching her to rope?"

"No. Her mother would kill me."

"She's learning anyway. Saw her a few days ago using a lasso."

Rudy frowned at the house, mumbled under his breath, cursing softly.

"She was good at it," Allan said.

"She'll pay for it, she doesn't keep it quiet. Her mother hates all that, hates the whole circuit; the people, the horses. I used to shower twice before I came back home to her. Never seemed to do much good."

Allan looked into the car, saw the saddle, the horse tack and worn-out ropes in the back seat. And he saw the duffle bag and thick army blanket and wondered how many nights Rudy spent on the road, in his car, the heater on against the cold outside.

"You're packed?" Allan asked.

"Mm? Yeah. I'll be hitting the road soon."

"Oh. I thought you were here for the winter. I thought there were no shows for a few months."

"Going to Nevada. There's always something in Nevada. I got a good chance at a big purse." Rudy smiled; a wide smile, wide enough to hide behind. "Shit, she used to hate it, me up and leaving, chasing purses around, chasing the big contests so she didn't have to worry about nothing. Boy she used to hate it."

"You mean Chloe or her mother?"

"Good question."

"Chloe know yet?"

Rudy bit his bottom lip and looked behind Allan, down the road, and watched a car come quietly through the snow, headlights barely cutting through the night as it passed them. The brake lights came on and they both turned to look at the car. It idled, warm, black, too dark to see inside and Allan's mouth dried, suddenly, and he had to pull hard to fill his lungs. He listened to the engine hum, the sound pushing at the wind, the snow moving quickly, nervously, away from the car, away from the heat. The door opened and a frail inch of laughter came out, light and flirtatious, and then Lori's long, stockinged legs and when she stood, shaking some thought from her hair, pulling her fur coat tight at the neck, Allan thought he was still a child next to her. She waved and laughed again before running up to the house. The car sat a minute but she didn't look back and after she had gone inside, turning on the lights, dropping her coat on the armchair, Allan looked back at the car, a long, low Ford and he tried to remember what kind of car Harris drove.

He looked back at Rudy.

"Nevada's a long way away."

"You got that right."

It was cold and the wind, that mean and hulking wind, laughed through the streets, silently turning the world to ice and Allan liked it. He walked home from work, in the dark, the wind cutting his flushed cheeks and thought it had been a while since he had been drunk, really drunk, so that he couldn't hear any words coming at him, so that he couldn't chase those thoughts anymore. He still had that eighty-dollar bottle of scotch he got himself for Christmas. He wondered where Lori would be.

Inside he left the lights off, made the drink in the dark, standing at the kitchen counter. Next-door the living room light was on and he could see the movement of the television beating at the window. He took his drink and went outside, out the front, without his coat and saw Chloe sitting on the curb again. He watched her, saw her breath mist in the air and swiftly dash away, chasing winter. After a minute he went and sat down next to her.

When she looked at him her eyes shone and he knew she had been crying the dry tears of what his father had called a rough and tumbler.

"How old are you?" he asked.

She watched him a minute. "Fifteen."

"Old enough, then." He held out his drink.

"What is it?"

"Scotch. Incredibly good scotch."

"That's what my father drinks."

"I know."

She took his glass and had a small sip. He could see her breath get taken away. "Not many cowboys drink scotch," she said. "Always go for bourbon or beer. Or both."

"And not many cowboys live among lawyers and bankers."

"He doesn't anymore."

"He did for a long time, though."

"I know," she said. "Still can't picture it."

"And I can't picture him on the road, riding bulls or whatever it is he does."

"He rides horses. Not bulls."

"I saw him. The other night. When he came to say goodbye."

"I didn't." She took another sip and handed the glass back to him and he waited for those eyes to wet up again. "We were at Wallace's parents' place. Stayed the weekend."

"Good time?"

"You bet. Mom and Wallace got drunk. Got to hear about what a loser my father is."

"Oh."

"It's okay. For a loser he sure wins a lot." When she smiled up at him, her eyes somehow wild, bristling, somehow very far away, he wanted to put his arm around her, hold her, keep her with him.

A small light came on across the street, in Parker's garage, and soon the smell of kerosene gripped the air and he knew Parker was standing at his workbench, looking out the window at the two of them. He liked the way the lamplight moved across the windowpane. He took another drink of the scotch and held the glass out and when she took it, watching him in that way young girls have, he looked down quickly, at her hands, and saw how rough they were already and he remembered all the roping she had been doing.

Later that night, while Lori slept, he went downstairs, padded around the house, looked through his records while he finished the scotch, alone. He liked the quiet way the night breathed when it was so late and later, when he went to the kitchen for another drink the moon was out, bright in the clear sky and he saw the girl standing in the backyard, holding the lasso limply in her hand, watching something in the darkness, watching something that wasn't there.

He took to stopping off at Oliver's for a drink on the way home. He'd sit at the bar and watch happy, breathless women let themselves be impressed by men who were a little too old, a little too sad but somehow expectant of the fawning, watch the way they cut so forcefully into Oliver's famous T-bones, watch the way they sipped so quickly at their drinks so the waiter seemed to always be with them. One night a woman sat close to him, smiled weakly behind her heavy black hair. She had dimples that made her look young and when she ordered a gimlet she drank it so easily, so needfully, that he ordered one as well. By her look she thought it was a come on and he let her, made small talk and thought about Lori and the way she had with Harris. When he left, walking home well past dark, his thoughts wandering around in gin, lost and happy about it, he realized that he smelled of the woman's perfume and was suddenly struck with guilt.

Lori was out and he showered, ate some toast, and then ran up to shower again before falling asleep on the sofa, listening to Nat King Cole sing about lonely men and later, when he woke, he saw Lori's coat by the front door and her purse in the kitchen. His head hurt and he had a glass of milk and went outside and watched Chloe's house. It was dark, sleeping, and he waited, half expecting her to come out to say hello.

There was snowstorm upon snowstorm and the world turned white, quiet, and disappeared. The banks closed, schools closed, and Allan stayed home and sat in the kitchen and listened to the radio, watched Lori cook, happily, smiling up at him every now and then and he wondered if she still liked having him around after all. He made coffee and took a strip of bacon that was cooling on a plate. Lori winked at him. She came close and he took her hand, pulled her to him and kissed her and when he saw the blue and red lights rolling silently over the snow outside he felt her go tense, felt her making the effort to stay so close to him. He let her go, smiled and looked back at the police cruiser pull into the driveway next door.

"What do you think happened?" he asked.

"You didn't hear?"

"Hear what?"

"She ran away?"

"Chloe?"

"That's right."

"When?"

"Two days ago. I think. Before the storms started. God, when do you think it'll stop? I'll have cabin fever by tomorrow."

"You look like you have it now," he said. "Two days ago?"

"You're always listening to that damned thing, have they said when it will all stop? When will you go back to work?"

"I don't know. Soon, I guess. Where do you think she went? Chloe, I mean."

"God knows. Somewhere without these damned blizzards.

"Maybe she went to Nevada."

She looked at him, wide-eyed and gone; far, far away and shook her head. "No. That's not far enough. Not for her."

It took Allan a few weeks to get used to her being gone, to get used to the quiet nights, to get used to the fact that the deep railroad of yelling was an afterthought from his own tired mind. It was her voice, the fighting, that he missed.

He bought a bottle of single malt he couldn't afford and walked home. It was warm and when he passed the Wilsons' home he smelled the gardenias blooming and he thought about sitting outside, on the front porch, listening to Nat King Cole, listening to 'Blue Gardenia', softly, quietly, so as he didn't wake Lori, didn't wake the neighbors.

Lori was home, reading in the living room and she smiled at him when he walked in, smiled wide and blank and his skin ran cold.

"What's in the bag?"

"Scotch."

"Ugh."

"I guess you don't want any, then?"

"No. I'm going out soon. With Claire. But thanks." She looked at him briefly as he set the bottle up on the dry bar, turned the bottle just so and walked away. "Not having one yourself?"

"I will later."

He ate dinner alone, at the kitchen counter, and when he smelled cigarettes he went outside to look for Chloe but forgot that she was gone. Spring had come on strong and the air was damp, smelled of turned soil, and somewhere, cigarettes.

It was early when he heard the yelling but he was awake anyway, downstairs, sitting at the piano, in the living room, the lights off, waiting for the daylight to break in the sky, to slowly spill into the living room, into the house. He smiled then remembered she was gone and listened harder. The voices were deeper, stronger, somehow sadder and he poured himself a fresh scotch. The yelling became screaming, a man's voice swearing to god and Allan took his drink outside, sat on his front steps. Thin streaks of red daylight crawled through the sky and the man's voice got louder and when a door slammed Allan saw something move across the street, in the Porters' upstairs window, and he wondered which of them was watching. He heard the familiar sound of Chloe's mother about to break. He took a sip of scotch and smiled. Rudy's Buick was parked at the curb. With the growing light he saw the mud and dust on the tires, kicked up on the mudguards and Allan wondered what part of the country had mud so red. Rudy came out of the house, his ex-wife's voice trailing after him, calling him a son of a bitch, a useless son of a bitch.

Rudy came down the stairs and stopped in their yard, then turned back. "You should have told me. The minute she was gone, you should have told me."

"You really expect me to think you would care?"

"What the hell else do you think I care about?"

When she screamed *Oh, just go away, just go away!* it was so loud, so hard, it spooked Allan, like the fight had jumped out at him from nowhere. The door slammed and Rudy kicked the tricycle so hard it hit the house. He turned around and looked up and down the street, his face cool and red in the dusty morning light. It was quiet, not even birds sang and Allan wondered if the fighting had scared them away. He watched Rudy pace, watched his body soften as the anger left and he walked slowly to the curb and sat down, lit a cigarette and took a deep drag, watching the sky and Allan tried to remember that Greek god with little wings at his feet.

Some Kind of Heaven

The hurricanes were different back then. There was more rain, more wind during the night, more laughter coming from eager faces and the news was always a step behind what was actually happening. It was the lead up I liked most of all, the quiet panic in the air, in the rain, the thoughtful heaviness of the oak trees and the way my mother laughed it all off, even though she always wanted to leave, run, head north to Memphis and I knew she was scared because of the way she held my hand too tight, even when she was sweating.

The night she met Raymond we only got the tail end, the good end, of a tropical storm that made landfall over in Galveston and wiped out half the town.

I heard them come home, heard her laughing, softly, nervously and I heard the delicate clatter of glass on glass as she fixed them another drink and I got out of bed and went out onto the balcony. The rain and the wind were heavy with salt from the Gulf and pulled at my clothes, at my hair and I looked down the balcony, part of it lit, making the rainfall shine bright silver in the light, until it disappeared out into the darkness, into the moss-covered southern oak in the park across the street. She laughed a lot and it made me nervous. I remembered the last time she had laughed like that, a few years ago, with a charmer. She made them another drink and I wondered how many she had had at the party, with Donald and Eleanor, who could hold their liquor. I watched the living room light reflect in the rain and when, an hour later, she let him out and turned off the lamp, the rain and the sky went dark. I waited, happy, in the dark, in the smashing rain and a few minutes later her bedroom light came on, at the far end of the balcony, and she stayed up for most of the night.

It was still raining in the morning and it looked like a sad, red dawn was setting in permanently, over the park, outside my window. The wind was very loud and reminded me of the sea. I could smell the cinnamon and eggs from the French toast my mother was making and knew she was in a good mood, knew she would be for a while, in that way when her skin seemed to radiate and her dimples blossomed and men stared at her with dumb, longing smiles and thought about hiding their wedding bands.

I went into the kitchen and asked if I could have a coffee.

"You're only eleven. It'll stunt your growth."

"But it smells so good."

"Doesn't the food?"

"It sure does."

"Then eat up, handsome."

"You're in a good mood this morning."

She looked at me over her coffee cup, her dark eyes shone so bright, so happy they almost looked electric. She smiled. "Did we wake you?"

"I was already awake. I couldn't sleep with all the wind."

"It's pretty nuts out there."

"We're lucky we didn't get hit hard," I said.

"We're always lucky."

A wet, rusty sun came through the clouds and lit the kitchen, lit my mother and she didn't even need to smile for me to see how happy she was.

"Must be a hell of a looker," I said.

"Oh yeah."

I watched her while I ate and she turned on the radio and found the weather report. The worst was over but Galveston was gone. In the apartment below John started to play piano, a broken, feeble rhythm and blues. He had been playing a few years, teaching himself, and I thought he should bite the bullet and get a teacher. I told him so once, when I met him on the stairs and he thought so too but never got around to it. But he had gotten better, if only just.

I didn't expect Raymond to be so handsome, and from his quiet lack of airs I don't think he expected it either. He should have smiled more, it looked good on him but he had a face where you knew they were few and far between, with a severe jaw and worried eyes that always looked like he needed more sleep. He came over the following night and my mother left us alone in the living room while she went and got dressed and he told me right off the bat he was nervous, he had never dated anyone with a kid before, at least not that he met. My mother had gone shopping for him, picked up some good bottled beer and he played with the bottle, ran his finger along the sweat and looked up at me now and then, worried, trying to think of what to say and when my mother came out, wearing a pretty blouse and miniskirt he tried not to stare.

"Do you work?" I asked.

"He does." My mother sat next to him. I felt like I was interviewing them. "And guess what he does, Lenny. He's a painter. Like your father."

"Your father is a painter?" he asked.

I pointed to a charcoal drawing of a woman that hung on our wall. Pinned up, the corners ruining.

"It's good," he said. He looked at me and blinked, his face marked with thin worry lines.

It was still raining when I watched them drive away, still cold like it gets after the hot, humid air gets torn apart by a storm and leaves everything fresh and quiet, but the wind was over and the rain fell straight and I leaned over the balcony and saw John, outside, right under me, watching them drive away as well. He flicked a cigarette out into the street and went back inside.

They came home late and she put on a record, and I heard her fix herself a drink and I heard his beer bottle gasp when he opened it. She talked a lot, quietly, just a mumbling murmur over the sad, singing voice of the record, and she laughed a lot and I strained to hear when Raymond talked but he was just too quiet. I heard her open the door from the living room to the balcony and I went outside, just out of the rain and I sat on the rough wood and watched the trees in the park and listened to them, listened to her, until she mentioned seeing his paintings and he stopped her.

"Look. I meant to say something. I led you on. I'm not that kind of painter. I don't know about art. I paint houses."

She laughed and told him that was okay, she had never been a cheerleader at LSU, they didn't take pregnant girls.

They went quiet and I knew they were kissing. I went back into my bedroom and tried to sleep and late that night I woke again and heard John, playing softly, downstairs, and I thought, yeah, he sure was getting better.

In the morning, when the park was still dark with dew and mist, before the street sweepers came by, singing and calling to each other, telling dirty jokes that I never understood, I stood on the balcony and looked into my mother's room and watched the two of them sleeping. She faced the window, her back to him, her legs kicked out from under the smooth sheet, her face lined at the forehead, thinking thoughts she avoided in waking hours. Raymond was out of sight, behind her, awake, his cigarette smoke showing as it caught the light.

Donald looked like he already had a few when we got to his house. His thick, silver hair was damp with the humidity, already out of place, and his laugh was loud and frequent and he kept eyeing my mother, telling her how great she looked, taunting his wife, smiling at my mother's legs as he took another drink of his gin, the sweat dripping from the glass to his shirt, making it look like he was lactating. Eleanor made a small fuss over me, straightening my tie, acting as though she liked children though my mother had told me some time before that Eleanor only liked the morphine she dosed herself with. But she smelled good, like soft skin cream and I was just old enough to notice how, when she bent over, her blouse fell open, showing her lingerie and delicate pink breasts. I told her I liked her hair and she smiled, touched my cheek and I felt myself blush.

We followed them through the house, out to the garden and I fell behind my mother and Raymond and saw she was holding his hand, tight, squeezing, talking a mile a minute, her eyes lit up and her voice husky and breathless, needing a drink. The pink vapor trails of sunset lit the garden softly in melted candy cane colors and made the guests look beautiful and charming as they laughed softly and drank quickly, the thin smell of alcohol fueling their talk. Donald turned on a record and the jazz he played was a little too loud, his eyes a little too flat as he watched his friends and he looked blankly toward my mother as she told a joke that wasn't very good and everyone laughed but Raymond, standing handsomely, quietly lost, behind her. He saw me watching him and he winked and went to get the two of them a drink.

"What do you think of your mother's new fellow?" Donald asked me. He handed me a soda and sat down on the back steps, next to me.

"He's better than the last one."

"So's a monkey. Want a cigarette?"

"I'm eleven."

"I was eleven when I started."

"Mom says I can't smoke until I'm thirteen."

"Get a note from your doctor."

"Your garden smells good."

"It smells like too many different perfumes getting tangled up. You should have been here yesterday. I had the place to myself. Grilled a steak, had a strong gin. It smelled good yesterday."

"Like steak and gin?"

"Like the best kind of quiet."

"Quiet has no smell."

"Says you. You aren't even old enough to smoke." He took a deep drag and blew the smoke up, away from me. "Handsome as anything, this Raymond. I don't trust people who are too good looking, especially men. There is little solid in such a handsome man."

"What do you mean solid?"

"They don't have to work as hard, try as hard, think as hard. So they don't end up hard."

I looked at Raymond, drinking a beer from the bottle, standing by my mother as she talked. He watched her and when her friends laughed at something she said, the corner of his mouth twisted slightly up, but it wasn't a smile.

"I don't know," I said. "He looks hard enough to me."

"He does, doesn't he? Makes me trust him less."

Raymond saw us watching him. He looked back for a minute, his face weary, his eyes tired and darkly ringed and there was another burst of laughter from the people next to him, their faces falling into the darkness as the sun disappeared and what little light there was faded out behind the tall sugar pines that lined the garden. He came over and stood beside us and looked at my mother and no one said anything though I felt Donald thinking.

"She's the life of the party, isn't she?" Raymond said.

"She doesn't know how not to be." Donald finished his drink in one swallow and excused himself for another.

They were out late again and I stayed up, waiting. I heard my mother, her laughter caught in the wind, coming from down the dark street, and wondered how Raymond made her laugh so much. I had never heard him even try a joke. She wore heels and I listened to the softly demanding clack and knew they were crossing the street, going into the park. The wind was strong that night. It rattled the balcony doors and moved hard through the trees down in the park, sounding cold and frustrated, and I turned off the lamp in the living room and stood at the balcony door, and looked across the street, at the park, tried to see my mother and Raymond, but it was too dark. I looked below me, at John's balcony, and saw him sitting in a chair, in the dark, in a corner, looking out at the park. His peculiar odor of sour, sleepless nights and the rank smell of the depressed got to me, made me feel trapped, made me panicked.

My mother shook me awake, smiling. The sunlight came through my window making her bright and beautiful and her eyes looked thrilled, like they did when married men flirted with her, and she told me to wake up, pack a bag, we were going on vacation, to the Gulf.

"How long?" I asked.
"In ten minutes."
"No, I mean how long we going for?"
"At least a week."

Raymond made us all scrambled eggs while my mother and I packed and after I watched him, hoping for a smile, but he was focused on the frying pan and on drinking his coffee. He looked at me and nodded from behind his mug and turned back to the eggs. He moved them in a pile to the side of the pan and added bacon.

As we drove toward the Gulf, across the state line and into Mississippi, the sun got hotter and I felt the salt in the air so much that my tongue seemed to dry out in my mouth. Raymond held my mother's hand and told her quietly that she could have her pick of the towns, that we would keep driving along the coast, going from town to town, from beach to beach, all the way to Florida if need be, until she found a place she was happy with. She smiled at him but he watched the road, his face tight against the white-hot sun, and kept looking up into the rearview mirror.

I slept on the sofa with the window open, the Gulf loud, laughing and full of the beckoning smells of the bottom of the seafloor, and late, when my mother and Raymond were asleep in the bedroom, their door shut but the hotel walls thin enough that in the quiet of the night I could hear their breathing, I went out, across the highway, and sat in the sand. There was no moon but the few bulking clouds seemed to feed off the light from the sea and I lay back, alone, on the beach and listened to the late-night sounds of the water and the lonesome cross-country trucks, hightailing it along the highway.

In the morning we ate fried crab at a breakfast shack on a pier that hung suicidally over the water and, later, while my mother lay out trying to get a good sunburn and I swam, Raymond watched the both of us from behind dark sunglasses, under a tree, up the beach, near the highway, chain-smoking and taking two hours to drink one warm bottle of beer, saying he didn't burn but just turned the meanest-looking brown you ever saw. I came out to dry off and my mother kept oiling her pink legs.

"That's gonna hurt," I said.

"But it looks good."

"I guess."

I lay down in the sun next to her. I could still smell the deep-fried seafood from the breakfast shack and the sun seemed to be burning the sea down to humid, salt-crusted air. My mother's hair was long and blew over to me, tickled the side of my face and reminded me of when I was a boy, about five or six, after my father had gone, and she used to sing to me every night, smiling, her big eyes hiding something and her beautiful, long hair that drove men so crazy touched my cheek and the softness put me to sleep.

I stood up and looked around. Palm trees lined the top of the beach, mile after mile, blowing mutely, almost ghost-like in the hot, lazy wind and I looked at the other people on the beach, young families and college kids, the heat getting to most of them, making them sweat and squint so they were worried-looking in their play.

"Where's Ray gone?" I asked.

"Back to the room. He's afraid of the sun." She closed her eyes and turned away from me, smiling, and she fell asleep, quickly and quietly and I wondered if I should cover her with something, stop the sunburn from getting out of control but she looked too happy and I went back into the water.

I fell asleep early, before dark, and dreamed I was still out in the water, watching the palms move in the wind, sure and steady, quiet in that way before hurricanes make landfall and I woke freezing cold, my own sunburn throwing my body out of whack. I lay on the sofa, trying to sleep, listening to the hushed, loving mumble of my mother and Raymond, talking, kissing, and when they went quiet and I was sure they were asleep, I took twenty cents from my mother's purse and went out, down to the hotel's soda machine. There was a purple mist glowing in the sky, lighting the hotel and the highway.

I sat outside our room, on the ground and drank the soda. Across the street the Gulf was inky and black but I knew it was moving, rolling. I heard my mother sigh inside the room.

"What's that sigh for?" Raymond asked.

"Just thinking."
"About?"
"Heaven."
"What's it like?"
"Quiet. Empty. Nobody there but me."
"Nobody at all?"
"Nobody at all."

I heard them moving, heard the thin sounds of the sheets against their clean skin, heard the thinking silence from Raymond and I knew he was smiling at my mother, still mostly confused by her.

"That's some kind of heaven," he said. The flint of his lighter scratched as he lit a cigarette.

"Your hair feels good."

I heard them kiss again and my mother moaned and I went back across the street to the beach. I sat close to the water and thought it was quiet, empty and nobody was there but me.

Raymond told us we hadn't gone far enough, we needed to get back in the car, back on the highway, and find another town, another beach, somewhere smaller, somewhere farther, where there weren't so many goddamned people. I voted for Florida.

His quiet, severe face looked nervous, thoughtful, in a way I had never seen, his eyes hung, dark and stained with exhaustion, but the muscle in his arms were tense and hard under the thin cotton of his shirt and I thought about what Donald had said, about handsome men not being hard. Raymond winked at me. It was as close to a smile as he could pull off. He looked back and forth from my mother's legs as she bent over packing the trunk of the car, to a gleaming, pale blue sedan that had come to the hotel overnight. He saw me watching him.

"Always wanted a car like that." He put on his sunglasses and hat. "Couldn't afford one though."

He drove slowly down the highway, cruising, taking his time, the Gulf a steamy green, parched in the afternoon, and my mother fell asleep in the front seat, her skirt high up on her leg, Raymond's hand resting above her knee. I fell asleep to the rolling hum of the car and woke later, sweating and thirsty, sure I was being watched, but I couldn't see Raymond's eyes behind his dark glasses.

"I'm hungry," I told him.

"You're mother's still asleep. If we stop we'll wake her."

"So?"

"She looks tired. She needs to rest."

"Okay."

When she woke, later, smiling and in a silly mood, saying she didn't want to sleep anymore, it was just death on an installment plan, Raymond pulled over at a motel and restaurant that looked dark and cool inside and promised the best air conditioning on the coast and two-for-one cocktails. There wasn't much of a town around it but the beach across the street was long and white and Raymond said the sand was the right color, it meant we were almost to Florida. They each had a Gibson, my mother eating both the onions, and they drank them fast and ordered another and my mother stirred hers with her finger, watching Raymond, a small hungry smile on her lips. He had taken off his hat but left the glasses on, and that, with the rough, blue shadow from not shaving that morning made him look somewhat menacing even though he opened his mouth, bared his teeth and tried to smile as my mother ran her foot along his ankle and thought I didn't notice.

We finished our steaks and they had coffee and my mother took one of Raymond's cigarettes from the package and lit it.

"Decide to take it up?"

"You make it look so good."

"Light one for me."

She did.

My mother and I waited in the restaurant while Raymond went to check us into the hotel, but he came back, forehead creased, a fresh cigarette going, and said there was no vacancy.

"But there's only a couple of cars in the lot," my mother said.

"Maybe the guests are out driving."

"The sign says vacancy."

"Fellow says it's been busted for years. This town's the pits anyway. Let's find somewhere a little nicer."

I said we should just go to Florida, we were almost there anyway.

When we drove out of the lot, back onto the highway, I saw one of the cars Raymond liked, one of the pale blue sedans he had been eyeing earlier and I pointed it out.

"Well, how about that," he said.

"This one was a Ford," I said. "Was the one this morning a Ford too?"

"Yeah. It was. Nothing beats a Ford."

He drove fast this time, saying he wanted to find somewhere pretty, somewhere with a good hotel and a pink sunset, before dinner. My mother leaned over and gave him a kiss and I told her to keep that stuff away from me.

It was called the Pink Sunset Hotel and Raymond told us it would do and though the sunset was blue and silver and setting behind us, over the western cleft of land the town sat on rather than out in the water, the town around was small, clean and busy with sunburned families, dressed up, out for the evening, happy in their beach-bred beauty.

"Are we in Florida?" I asked.

"We drove through Pensacola while you slept."

"What's that mean?"

"It means, yeah, we're in Florida."

"Good."

Before dark I went for a swim in the empty silver sea and it was cool enough, the sun was low enough, that Raymond sat on the beach with my mother. There were a few other swimmers in the water, older teenagers, the boys loud, moving fast and wild, impressing the girls who weren't much older than me and I watched the girls and liked how their wet skin looked so hard but so smooth.

Raymond stood, his long pants and shoes out of place on the beach, and waved for me to come in.

Later, while Raymond was in the shower getting ready for dinner, I smelled his cigarettes and found my mother outside, standing in the dark, away from the tropical neon lights of the hotel sign, smoking one of his cigarettes.

"Since when do you smoke?" I stood next to her and had a good view of the bare, dark water, swollen and sad-looking. People passed by out on the street, lit and loud but out of focus.

"Doctors say it's good for the nerves."

"What's wrong with your nerves?"

"God knows."

She put her arm around my shoulders and hugged me, kissed my hair and told me she loved me. I could smell the sun on her skin. She dropped the cigarette, put it out with her heel and we went to get Raymond and the three of us walked down the main drag, across from the beach, the lights bright, the drunken tourists' smiles brighter and we had southern fried fish for dinner at a small place, one of the few without come-hither lighting and the loud rumble of too many voices.

When I woke up my mother was gone. The bedroom door was open and I stood in the doorway and looked at Raymond while he slept, his face calm and handsome with the living, dusty copper sunlight that shone through the open window, and the crying sound of the sea echoed across the highway. The sheets had been pulled tight where my mother had slept. Raymond turned and reached his arm out, trying for my mother, but took a pillow instead and he pulled it close to his chest. He needed to shave. I could hear his beard scratching against the pillowcase. The ashtray sat on my mother's bedside table and it looked like she had been up most of the night, alone, smoking, stubbing them out before they were finished. I shut the door to let Raymond sleep in. This time he looked like he needed it.

Outside the wind blew, still cool with dawn, still heavy with the burned salt smell of the Gulf. A man in a tuxedo walked by the hotel, by our room, his face lost in the earliness of the hour, an empty green champagne bottle in his hand, hanging, like he wanted no part of it.

I crossed over to the beach, squinting in the sunrise, looking for my mother, a brisk chill cutting the air, running down my neck. The beach was empty of people and the thoughtful sea looked tired, salted and smoked by the long summer.

It rained that night and I slept well enough, listening to it come and go, hitting the window, and to the muted, watery sounds of the tourists outside, running to their drinks. I woke when I heard my mother laughing excitedly, late, after the bars had closed and the revelers gone to sleep, and I went to open the bedroom door but Raymond was alone. He sat by the open window, his back to me, tapping an unlit cigarette on the armrest. The wind moved the curtains softly and I heard the wet sound of a long-haul truck's wheels out in the highway. Raymond lit the cigarette, blew the smoke toward the window and turned to look at me, his face thoughtful.

"Go back to bed, Lenny. Try to get some sleep."

"I heard her laughing."

He shook his head at me.

"Go to sleep. I'll ask around at sun up. Someone will have seen her."

I spent the day in the hotel's lobby, watching the storm clouds over the gulf and reading in the newspaper about a hurricane that was expecting to make landfall sometime in the evening, over toward home. The woman behind the counter gave me quick, sad looks most of the day and Raymond came and went, talking to anyone who would listen and I got the feeling that if we stayed in town too long he would become known as the village idiot.

When, two days later, the sun came out hot and high and I went to the beach in the morning, I thought I saw her again but it was a young girl, little older than me, running after her parents. Her laugh was the same too; excited, teasing, full of a shyness I didn't buy, but many men would. Raymond watched me from behind his glasses and when he spoke his voice was hoarse from smoking too many cigarettes.

That night we went out for dinner and ate in the beachfront patio of one of the string of brightly lit restaurants. Sunburned women walked by, on the sidewalk, smiling at Raymond, slowing down when they saw him and the air was thick with salt, fried food and cold beer. Raymond had finally shaved and he had made me bathe, and he ordered two sirloins for us, smiling at the waitress, but there was nothing in it. He looked at me and took a sip of iced tea.

"She's not coming back, is she?"

"No." He shook his head. "I don't think she is."

Raymond's handsome face tightened. The waitress came back and refilled our water glasses, looking down at me, smiling at me and it made me think of the way Donald smiled at my mother after he had had a few and had become deaf to Eleanor and I thought about how, later, when we walked home from their parties, my mother would grab my hand tight, nervous about something and I knew she wanted to leave, run, go somewhere quiet and empty.

Muddle Through

They left the show early. Roy wanted to stay, to see the clowns, to see the woman come back on her horse, her pretty hair dancing behind her, but he didn't say anything. They ate hot dogs and mustard at a bench, under a tent that smelled of peanuts, and watched the rain. It was dark and the red lights and fire from the torches flickered and shone as people ran huddled and laughing from tent to tent, show to show. The rain built up, slapped into the earth and dust and, when a small brown bear walked by, led by a skinny, sour-looking man, Roy could smell the dampness in the animal's fur. When there was a roar of laughter and applause, Roy knew he had missed some good clowns.

That night they slept in the car. The cuffs of Roy's jeans were wet and it was cold enough that they took all night to dry and when they did they were stiff and sharp against his ankles. He woke a lot during the night. When trucks drove past, their tires sucking at the wet highway, Roy watched his breath move like liquid pearl in the air. He remembered her hair. She had had pretty hair.

Frankie pushed in the lighter and waited.

"Go to sleep, Roy."

"Yes, sir."

He watched Frankie smoke his cigarette, quietly, in the dark, his seat pushed back, the smoke curling very slowly out of the inch of open window. The rain patted down on the car. It grew stronger and the metallic hum made Roy sleepy. Organ music still rang in his ears.

"Go to sleep." Frankie flicked his cigarette butt out the window. The clouds had cleared in the north. Cold, silver shadows lit the sky and Roy could see Frankie's face in the dark. Frankie looked down at him and tried to smile.

When he woke, they were on the road. The sky was a deep and dusty blue with rolling storm clouds that looked like charcoal bricks, but the rain was gone. Frankie rolled down his window.

"Where we going?" Roy asked.

"Kansas," Frankie said. "That knife thrower you liked, back in Vermont, she told me about a place in Kansas."

Roy nodded and looked out the window.

Their first night in Kansas they went to the show and it was very quiet. Wind dry as bone dust blew through the fairground and carried the smell of the animals, of perfume and kerosene. Roy watched two boys, smaller than him, still holding their mothers' hands while a Russian juggled fire. The flames moved in the air, roaring quietly, throwing a deep a red light on the juggler's face. He saw the lines between his eyes and the deep, hollow cheeks filmed with sweat and thought the Russian was getting too old. Frankie called him and they went into the big top.

The ringmaster was tall and had a throaty, haunted-sounding voice, his requests more like commands. The small audience was pulled in, but he was too serious, his voice too foreboding for his own jokes. Roy fell asleep during the high-wire act, his head pressed into Frankie's shoulder, smelling the cigarettes and cold air that came from his clothes. When the woman came out, doing a handstand on a horse, Roy felt Frankie go tense and woke up. He looked up at him as Frankie watched the woman, frowning.

"I'm hungry," Roy said.

Frankie took a bill from his wallet. "Find out where the acts are eating. I'll catch up."

Roy stopped to watch a clown that had come on. The clown kept talking, sounding angry, pushing out the words, hard, trying to force a laugh. Roy wanted to tell him not to speak, that any clown worth his salt knew not to speak, but he turned away.

"Roy," Frankie called. "Keep an ear out for work. We might have to stop a bit."

Roy nodded. He left the tent, weak laughter dying quickly behind him.

He walked past the games and stopped at the duck shooting. A thin woman with heavy red hair was laughing as she looked down the sights of the BB gun. She said something and the clerk laughed uncomfortably and stood back. Roy watched her shoot, hitting the metal ducks, once each, quickly, smiling as she went. She turned, smiled down at him, and asked if he wanted a turn. He told her he wanted something to eat, asked her where she would go.

"Where would I go?" She laughed. Her skin was very pale and looked like it would be cold to the touch. The strings of lights swung easily in the wind and flashed through her hair. Roy wanted to touch it. "I'd go to Orpheo's steakhouse, in Manhattan. That's where I'd go."

"How about if you were walking?" Roy asked.

"There's a food truck next to the mirrors." She pointed.

"You eat there?"

"No." She smiled. She showed a lot of teeth, ran her tongue across them, and he tried to tell if that was familiar. "Near the back. By the stables. Just follow the smells. Horses and hamburgers."

He buttoned his coat and pulled up the collar. The air smelled of firewood and horse shit. When the wind blew strong enough, he couldn't hear the circus.

He ate alone. Three men sat at a table across from him, eating, talking a little, grunting at small jokes. They were dressed like the lumberjacks he had seen when he and Frankie had gone through Oregon. One of them stared back at Roy and, when Roy didn't break away, the man nodded slightly and smiled. A calliope started up somewhere and the men groaned at each other.

"They've heard that damned calliope too much." A man dressed in a tuxedo sat down next to Roy. He wore black-rimmed glasses and he smiled slyly and Roy thought he looked like a TV show presenter he had seen once. He held out a hand for Roy. "Will Powers, mind reader. On at five, seven, and nine but no one comes to the nine o'clock. Or the seven."

"I thought the gates open at five-thirty."

"They do. I think someone's trying to screw me."

"You should know."

"You mean my being a mind reader and all?"

"Sure."

"Hell, you're surly as those guys." He nodded toward the men across the table and picked up a French fry.

"Surly?"

"Gruff." He took a bread roll and put it on Roy's tray. "Who you looking for?"

Roy looked at him.

"It's not mind reading, you just got that look. You study every face that walks by out there."

"I can have this roll?"

"Why you think I put it on your plate?"

"Thank you."

Roy saw Frankie in the crowd, thin, dark, and tired. He was squinting against the bright lights. Two women holding their daughters' hands kept looking at him as they passed. They were both blonde and pretty and their dresses looked perfectly ironed. Frankie watched a horse turning in nervous circles and then scanned the crowd.

"Frankie," Roy called out. He waved. Frankie saw him, looked back at the horse, and walked to the table. He looked at Roy's plate.

"Come on," he said.

They walked through the small crowds, through the lights, the calliope getting louder. Frankie stopped at a cart that was popping corn and bought a box, told the man to make sure it was a warm one.

"I told you before, you should be calling me dad." Frankie held the popcorn out for Roy. The wind turned roughly, rippled the sawdust and dirt over the ground and Frankie watched the sky. Roy thought he looked worried, but it was hard to tell.

They stayed in a boarding house north of town that offered a good weekly rate. Their room was on the third floor, next to the stairs. At night, when the sky was clear, Roy could see the ruby-red glow of the circus over the trees and in the sky. It was getting cold, but Frankie slept with the window open, said he needed the air, and come morning, Roy was usually pressed into Frankie's back for the heat. When Roy got out of bed and washed his face at the sink, he saw Frankie was awake.

"Brush your teeth before you go downstairs."

"Yes, sir."

"Stay near the house today."

"I will."

Frankie found work at the railyard. He left early and came home late, after supper, when the rest of the boarding house had gone to bed and Roy could hear the other guests, in their rooms, their radios on, smoking cigarettes and drinking by themselves, the sound of a bottle softly hitting a glass tumbler easing down the hall. When Frankie got in, he made Roy take the first bath.

"I don't want one."

"You're not sleeping in that bed, dirty as you are."

"Why don't you go first?"

"I'm covered in coal dust. You want to bathe in coal dust?"

After, Frankie turned out the light and sat in the chair by the window, smoking, watching the lights over the circus. They could hear the murmur of a radio from downstairs.

"We going back on Saturday?" Roy asked.

"Going back tomorrow. After work. Friday is always a good day to go."

"Last week I met a woman that could shoot better than anything."

Frankie put out his cigarette and sat back. Outside the wind was quite strong and pressed against the house. A cold, prairie moonlight came through the window and gently lit the room, missing Frankie, keeping him in sharp shadows, but Roy knew Frankie was watching him.

Roy saw her from behind, in the dark, behind one of the big tents. Her hair was pulled back tight, in a smooth red ponytail that caught the small light and made him thirsty. She was incredibly thin. She took her foot in hand and brought it up to her face and over her head, slowly, like a dancer, her toe pointed. She bent it backward and Roy winced at the sight. Her breath showed pale in the cold air. The dusty earth swayed softly at her feet, pulled to and fro by the wind. She saw him watching and smiled. Dimples broke through her white, pristine skin and he thought they made her look goofy, like an awkward bird in a cartoon he had seen once, some time ago.

Frankie walked up behind him and stopped, lit a cigarette, and shook out the match. He took a long pull and put a hand gently on Roy's shoulder.

"She's pretty," Frankie said.

Roy nodded. The woman watched Frankie, her expression playful.

"Let's go. High wire starts soon."

It was cold that night and Roy felt winter coming. He watched boys with red cheeks and cropped hair run through the fairgrounds, laughing, yelling, full of bluster, their skin raw with fresh air and the threat of frost. Frankie took his hand and pulled Roy quickly through a crowd, nodding familiarly to an usher who blinked blankly at him. Frankie's hand was tender and Roy felt the bruising in his palms, the calluses worn soft from the railyard. Red and gold lights flashed over the faces in the crowd and they went to sit high up in the stands.

They stayed until the end of the show and went to eat, at the back, near the stables, where it was quiet. Frankie watched Roy eat and took a bit now and then off his plate.

"Get your own," Roy said.

Frankie smiled. He tapped his ear and told Roy to listen.

"What?"

"Christmas carols. On the radio behind the counter."

"It's too early for Christmas carols."

"It's never too early."

They went back on Sunday, in the afternoon. Sunlight struck sharply from a clear, quiet sky and small dust devils kicked up the ground, blowing dirt, hay, and dry, chalky manure up to their knees. Once, when a woman with red hair Roy thought was a wig and bright, Irish blue eyes smiled at Frankie, he held Roy's hand tight enough to hurt and quickened his step.

They went for lunch at a restaurant down the road from the fairground and, when Frankie went to the counter to order, the mind reader sat down in front of Roy. He took off his glasses to clean them and smiled at Roy.

"Wise move, son. Food's better here. And you can't smell the horses."

"I don't mind the smell of horses."

"That your dad?" Powers nodded toward Frankie, his back to them, talking to the counter girl, making her laugh.

"Yeah."

"Doesn't look like you."

"I look like my mother."

"Yeah, I'm the same."

"No. I know who you look like," Roy said. "You look like Steve Allen. The one from television."

Powers laughed quietly. Behind him, at the counter, Frankie watched Roy in the mirror with dark, careful eyes. He nodded and sat down on a stool, turned over a coffee cup and the girl came to fill it.

"You ever have a lady ringmaster?" Roy asked.

"A lady ringmaster? No, not that I know of. But I've only been around a year. I was up in Alberta before this. It was too cold to stay up there."

"I saw one, this one time, a while back."

"You're too young to have 'a while back' for anything."

"Well, I saw her. She did the best show you've ever seen."

"You've seen enough to know?" Powers laughed.

"I've seen enough. I've seen a lady ringmaster. How many people you know seen a lady ringmaster?" Roy's chest grew tight and his voice took a rough, venomous edge. Powers smiled at him, worried behind his glasses.

"I've never seen one."

"No," Roy said.

"Ben," Powers turned around in his chair and poked the roughneck sitting behind him with a finger. "Ben. You ever hear of a circus that had a lady ringmaster?"

"Yeah. We did. Couple years back. She moved north. Maybe Michigan."

"She any good?" Roy asked.

"I liked her. A little on the wild side, but the crowd ate it like caramel corn. Think she pissed the clowns off, but they're a touchy bunch."

Powers smiled, "How about that? You were right."

They got back to the rooming house late that night. It was cool and the air smelled of falling leaves and dry grass. A light was on downstairs. Frankie turned off the engine and they looked at the glowing window, small against the wide, black, empty sky. Frankie had bought Roy a candied apple and the sugar had melted, sticking to Roy's lips and cheeks enough that he wanted to wash.

They went in and started up the stairs. They heard a radio in the living room and the lamp threw a soft, ruddy light into the hallway and spilled over the bottom of the stairs.

"Who's that?"

"It's Frankie, Miss Wryson."

The floor moved under her weight as she came to the door. She wore a man's housecoat and her hair hung straight, down to her shoulders. It was blacker than Frankie's and when she smiled, mockingly and haughty, Roy thought she looked like a raven.

"Number twelve and son," she said.

"Yes," Frankie said. "Number twelve."

"You should have a drink with me. I have this whole bottle all to myself. You'd be better company than the radio."

"Don't know about that. What's on?"

"It was Gershwin. The program was meant to go for the hour, but there's some news bulletin they stopped it for."

"Oh? What'd they say?"

"The usual. Cops and robbers. I don't know. How about that drink?" Her voice became soft, thick in the throat. "Send the little one up to bed."

"Another time, Miss Wryson. It's been a long day."

"Another time."

She stayed in the doorway and watched them go up the stairs, ice ringing in her whiskey glass. The man on the news spoke quietly and severely, but Roy couldn't make out the words.

Roy washed his face in the sink. The cold water seemed to harden the candy on his lips. He watched Frankie in the mirror, sitting down by the window, the small lamp burning brightly next to him, the curtains open and moving weakly in the little wind that came through the window. Roy fell asleep easily but woke often to look at Frankie sitting in the dark, blowing his cigarette smoke out the window, his dark eyes bright with the stars in a clear sky. The wind that came into the room was cold and when Roy woke again, very late, the house was dead silent. He watched Frankie, watched the red bud of light from the cigarette swell when he took a pull.

"Get some sleep, Roy."

He woke again before dawn. Frankie sat on the side of the bed, looking down at him. He told him to get dressed.

It was still dark when they got back onto the highway, but the stars had the hushed, dim quality of daybreak. Cold red and blue vapor trails veined the edge of the sky, looking like cotton candy, crawling out of the darkness of wheat fields. They kept their windows all the way down and at a rail crossing the gate was lowered, the red light blinking silently. They waited and when the train came they sat back and watched it like they were at a drive-through. The last string of boxcars had *Montana* written across them and the hot smell of metal burning into metal filled the raw morning air. Frankie smiled at the train and Roy tried to remember when he had last seen him smile like that.

They drove through Missouri, listening to the rain beating on the car's roof. The rhythm of the windshield wipers made Roy sleepy and the road ran darkly in front of them. Roy wanted to turn around, stay longer in Kansas.

"It's better we keep moving," Frankie told him. "Turn on the radio. Find us some music."

"Not the news?"

"Not the news. I'm tired of the news." He rolled down the window a little and put his cigarette, still only half smoked, through the gap. Rainwater streamed in and the air smelled fresh and like wet farmland. Lightning silently cut through the sky and Roy counted for the thunder. When it came it was muted, the sound swallowed up by the thrashing rain.

He tuned the radio dial until a woman sang out to him. It was a Christmas carol and he sat back, looked at Frankie, proudly, like he had given him the carol personally. She had a sad, deep voice and when the song ended and a man started to speak, Frankie switched off the radio.

"That was real good," Roy said.

Frankie nodded. "That was Judy Garland."

"I want to hear it again."

"You will."

They ate at the counter. Coming in from the road, the rain had been severe and they sat dripping on their stools. The rainwater caught the dust from their clothes and pooled at their feet. Roy looked through the records in the Wall-O-Matic. Behind the counter, the grill hissed while the cook listened to the radio up on a shelf, watching eggs cook, his hard, scrubbed face blank and worried.

The cook set down their plates and looked at them. "Been on the road long?"

"Since Kansas."

"Kansas?" He looked up at the radio again and nodded to it. "You hear what happened out there? You hear about the lady that was killed? In her own home. Somebody just walked in and shot her down in her very own home."

"I didn't hear." Frankie said.

"I'll turn it up so you can hear. The news goes the full hour."

"Okay."

They watched the cook walk away, stopping briefly to turn the volume on radio. Kansas was still making the news.

"Eat up quick," Frankie said.

Roy nodded and cut into his pancakes.

It was snowing when Roy woke up. The car windows were closed and Frankie ran the heater. The tender, silver luster of morning melted into the edge of the sky. Late autumn leaves scrapped and scattered across the road. Roy smelled their wet clothes in the back seat, smelled the wet denim and fresh mud and he tried to remember what he had done with his shoes. He looked up at Frankie. In the early morning light, he looked very young, too young to be a father, too young to be so worried.

The snowfall grew heavy. The sky darkened in an ominous manner and pressed down on them like a weighted slate, the flakes caught the little oyster-white light still in the sky and shone very brightly. Frankie turned the heater up. Their breath misted and the windows started to show steam in the corners.

"Don't know when we saw snow last," Roy said.

Frankie nodded. "Before your grandmother died."

"When was that?"

"Couple years ago."

"Guess that's a long time." Roy looked out the window.

Frankie looked at him and punched in the lighter. He took a cigarette from the pack in his pocket and placed it on his lips.

"You want to stop?" Frankie asked.

"I'm not hungry yet."

"I don't mean for breakfast."

Roy squinted at a rough line of pink in the breaking sky and bit his lip. Fir trees lined the road and the snow caught in their dark branches.

Frankie looked at him, waiting. The lighter popped and he lit his cigarette, blinked the sleep away from his eyes and turned on the headlights. The snow flashed, moving quickly in the yellow beams and back out into the dark morning.

They stopped outside of Grand Rapids and stayed at the Sleeping Bear Motor Court. Frankie made Roy soak in the bath and went back to the office to talk to the manager and, when Frankie shut the door and passed the window, Roy got out of the tub and went to watch the changing neon lights of the hotel's sign, the bear sleeping and winking, his sleeping cap moving from side to side. He opened a window and the snow blew in off the windowsill. The air smelled of cut pine and fish. He heard the office manager laughing and wondered since when did Frankie tell jokes. Later, when Frankie came back into the room, quietly, thinking Roy would be asleep, Roy could smell the whiskey on him even from the bed.

Frankie kept the light off and drew the curtains, leaving only a few inches open and sat down at the table by the window and watched the bear while he smoked a cigarette. His face shone briefly with the red and yellow from the sign. When he put out his cigarette and looked over at Roy, Roy tried to look asleep, even though Frankie always knew. Outside, the sign powered down and the lights went out. A pale, icy winter light came from the stars and silver shadows settled over Frankie's face, showing the line in his brow. He lit a fresh cigarette and smiled over at Roy.

"Manager saw a show two weeks ago. Said the ringmaster was the prettiest redhead he'd ever set eyes on."

"Where?"

"Eighty miles on."

"Think they're still there?"

"Yeah."

"When will we go?"

"Thursday."

"Thursday is a good day."
"Yeah, Thursday is a good day."

The snow made it look like a ghost town. An organ played Christmas carols, but the wind hollowed out the sound, made it distant and harsh, like the sound of a faraway freight train. A woman played the violin, under an open tent, a lamp flickering deep yellow firelight over her face. Roy stopped, watched her, watched her mouth and saw she was singing but too quiet to hear. Next to her, a bare-chested man was cleaning his swords, rubbing them down with a white cloth and alcohol, the sterile, antiseptic smell catching in the wind. Frankie put his hand on Roy's shoulder.

"Let's go. I'm hungry. They got hot dogs in the big top."

They ate in the stands and watched the clowns' warm-up act. The spare, scattered audience didn't clap, didn't seem to notice, but the clowns kept going anyway, chasing their tails, doing it well. When an usher walked up to them and said to sit anywhere, it was going to be a quiet night, they went close and Roy saw the clowns were smiling, finding themselves funny even if the crowd didn't.

"I'm still hungry," Frankie said. "And these are good. Go find that hot dog girl and get us two more. Lots of mustard, lots of onions."

When the show started, they sat up straight. Three dark-haired women, Romanian triplets, came out on angry, blustering mares, and Roy saw the last girl, her face and her smile tight and hard, holding the reins taught, trying to control the horse, trying to follow the other two. Her thin body was tense and her deep, coal-black hair moved swiftly, almost sweetly, through the air, the length of her ponytail waving with the turning horse. Roy wondered which one was new, the mare or the Romanian.

The candy girl came around and Frankie waved at her. She gave him a smile, a little too long and a little too wide, and

Roy wondered if they knew each other. Her black stockings ran at her thin ankles and her pale, wheat-looking hair hid the sides of her face so that she could only see you straight on. When she came and sold Frankie a box of popcorn, smiling at him, goofy and flustered, she looked around, decided she had nowhere else to be and sat down with them. She reached across Frankie, gave Roy a candy cane and winked at him. Her smile was a little crooked and Roy thought she looked like his grandmother, after the stroke, when her mouth twisted up every time she tried to speak.

Frankie nodded toward the ring. "It's a good show."

"Not tonight it's not," she said. She leaned forward on her candy tray. "It's dead tonight. You'll have to come back in a week or two. It'll be better. Half our people are away. That's why the lions won't come out tonight. They're moody when the boss is away."

"Worse than the clowns?"

"Worse than the clowns," she said. She gently touched her hair and looked at Frankie. Her eyes were very wide and very blue and Roy thought she hadn't had much sleep, not for a long time. "I feel like I know you."

Frankie looked at her and shook his head.

"Maybe I've been spending too much time with that reincarnated fortune teller." She sat back and put her legs up on the seat in front of her, crossing them at the ankles, snow-caked sawdust and dirt falling from her slippers.

Frankie looked down at Roy, worried. He took a cigarette from his shirt pocket and put it in his mouth. "I'm going outside for a minute."

The girl watched him go.

Later, when they drove back to the motor court, neither spoke. Roy watched the moon between the haunted blackness of the pine trees along the road, the light coming in lonesome-looking flashes of pearly smoke. It had been a long show and they were tired. They had lingered after the final act, their jackets buttoned up and collars turned against the nighttime wind that blew through the stands. Roy stood close to Frankie and smelled the cigarettes and shaving cream on his skin. The lights went out and an exhausted juggler in a fur coat was walking from torch to torch, snuffing the flames. The snow had melted already, but Roy thought that the frozen dirt underfoot looked colder than snow, the white cracks of frost breaking through the earth. As they left, Roy saw the candy girl, standing near the ticket booth, watching Frankie. She waved goodbye with her fingers when he looked up at her. After they got in the car, Frankie punched in the lighter, but when it popped, he didn't light a cigarette. Moonlight played across his face and he looked over at Roy.

They had blueberry pie and coffee in the all-night restaurant across from the Sleeping Bear. Silver Christmas tinsel hung around the windows of the motel's office, and it caught the flickering red and yellow light of the bear sign. Someone had put a pine wreath on each door along the motor court.

"No ringmaster," Roy said. "Never seen a show without a ringmaster."

"Half their people were away. Their boss was away."

"So we'll go back?"

"We'll go back."

Roy went to bed and Frankie stayed up, by the window, open an inch to catch the cigarette smoke. Roy watched him from the darkness of his covers, watched him slowly play the cigarette across his lips, tap it on the package sitting on the table. He didn't light it, not while Roy was awake. His face was calm and thoughtful and Roy could see his breath mist thickly against the bleak, silver glare of the moon on the windowpane. Before dawn, Roy woke briefly and saw Frankie was not in the room, not at the window or in the bed next to him. The room lit up, a pallid beam of light ran across the ceiling as a truck went by, out on the highway. Roy held onto a pillow and went back to sleep.

The snow fell all week. At night the wind picked up, came in off the trees, and carried the feel of the ice that grew in their branches and the tar smell of their sap. And in the mornings, before Frankie went into Grand Rapids for the day, for work, they had pancakes at the restaurant across the road. They ate slowly and when Frankie leaned back, still holding his coffee cup on the table, an arm over the back of the booth, Roy tried to do the same. A school bus passed them out on the road and Frankie looked at it and blinked, coming out of thought.

Roy sipped his orange juice. "When we going back?"

"Next week. She said they'll be back next week."

They went to town, to the movies. Roy watched the picture and thought it wasn't as good as a real show, as a circus. But it made Frankie laugh, quietly, his cigarette moving in his mouth as he smiled. Roy wondered why he was laughing and thought the clowns were funnier, even bad clowns.

"Put your feet on the floor, Roy."

"Yes, sir."

Frankie sat back and Roy looked up, at the shadows moving across his face, at the cigarette smoke coiling through the gray light. In the seats below them, a man murmured into a brunette's ear and she moved away, smelling of perfume and hairspray. The man put on his hat and walked out of the theater, coughing and glaring at the carpet as he went, his face sour. Roy turned to watch the man leave and saw the woman watching him. She smiled, waved her fingers at him and stood up and, as she walked up the aisle toward him, he thought she was skinny enough not to make a difference to the projector. She sat down next to him and smoothed her skirt. When Frankie looked at her, his dark eyes squinting, she smiled and sat back and watched the rest of the movie with them. Roy tried to sit still and when he sat up and put his hand on the armrest, he touched her hand and thought it was very cold and very soft. Frankie used a cigarette to light a second and Roy wondered why the girl wound him up. He hadn't seen him like that for a while, not for over two years, he thought.

When the movie ended, she looked at Frankie, tilted her head lazily, and stretched, giving him a modest smile. Her eyes were wide, a soft pale brown that reminded Roy of baked honey he had eaten when he was in Montana, at a fair, a long while ago. Frankie didn't smile back at her and she turned her head slightly, her long, lank hair hiding her face. When the lights came on in the theater and the curtain closed over the screen, the lights weaving through the thick, red velvet, Frankie stood and said they were going for hot dogs, did she want to come.

"You bet, brown eyes." She smiled at Frankie, and as Roy stood, she looked at him, winked, and smoothed his hair.

They walked through a fine, dark snow. The shop windows were dark, the occasional Christmas display brightening the bare streets with golden bells and twitching red and green lights. The café on the corner was empty but for one table of men who looked long and hard at the girl and quickly at Frankie. Steam laced the windows. The girl took Roy's hand and they walked to the back, sat in a booth by the window. Frankie looked out at the street, at the snow and the flat, metallic sky. He smiled at Roy and at the girl; calmly, happily, and Roy saw something in Frankie's eyes, far back in the dark, skittish, like a horse about to burst.

They ate steamed frankfurters and French fries. The girl sat close to Roy, close enough he felt the hardness of her hipbone. She leaned into the table, watching Frankie, smiling at him all the time, even when he didn't say anything.

"I know you. I've seen you before," she said. "You ever been to Wisconsin?"

"We've passed through." Frankie dipped his frankfurter in mustard.

"Three, four years ago?"

"No."

"Where you from?"

Frankie looked quickly at Roy and out the window again. "Out west. Haven't been back in a while, though."

"So, is it just the two of you?"

"We're going to meet up with Roy's mother."

"Oh." She took a French fry and smiled tightly at Roy. When she turned away and let her hair hide her face, Roy saw her in the windowpane, warped and silver, a car's headlights flashing over her worried eyes. "Good. A boy needs his mother."

"How long you been with the circus?" Roy asked.

"Three, almost four years."

"Three, four years selling candy and cigarettes? That's nuts."

"I moonlight."

Roy shook his head.

"Next time you come, get your fortune told. I'm good at it."

"You're the fortune teller?" Roy asked. "But you said before that you've been spending too much time with the fortune teller."

She smiled at him and smoothed his hair. Her touch was very gentle. When she ran the back of a finger on his cheek, softly, he smelled the cold cream on her skin.

They went early and walked around, watched the sideshows and ate popcorn, and when it grew dark and the lanterns were turned on, they watched young faces glow warmly, smiling open-mouthed at the sword swallower. The ground was damp from melted snow. Roy's boots stuck slightly with each step. A woman walked by, red hair waving swiftly in the cold, leading two camels into a tent, their long necks swaying. Frankie looked at her and took Roy's hand. They walked past the fortune teller and she smiled. She looked different in costume, older and sadder, a look that Roy saw in Frankie, late at night, when he couldn't sleep. He waved at her. The air was very dry and powdered snow blew from the tops of the tents, catching the amber from the lights. Someone was singing Christmas carols.

"What was her name?" Roy asked.

"You know that."

"No. The lady on the radio. She sang that carol."

"Garland. Judy Garland."

"Yeah."

Frankie looked down at Roy. A boy ran past, laughing, an older girl chasing him, mud splashing up the back of her heavy, white stockings. Two policemen walked through the crowd, smiling, nodding, the older of the two touching his hat now and then. They stopped to have their fortunes told and Roy saw the girl take hold of a palm, touching it with a soft finger. The cop said something that made her smile and tilt her head in small laughter.

They went into the big top and sat high up in the stands. It was crowded already. A clown was playing the piano. He was quiet and focused, not playing it up for laughs.

When the ringmaster came out, she rode a shining, walnut horse. She rode him well, her bare thighs pressed hard against it, her hand waving smoothly, her red hair bouncing happily behind her. She stood on the saddle.

Frankie leaned back and crossed his feet. He looked down at Roy and roughed up his hair, smiled darkly with tired eyes. Roy watched the ringmaster jump easily from the horse. She took the microphone and her voice was smooth and laughing. She teased the men in the close seats, made them blush with a coy look and a hungry smile. When the clowns came back on, Roy saw Frankie was asleep, his chin in his chest, his arms crossed in front of him.

At intermission they went outside. Frankie lit a cigarette and looked at the crowd flowing through the tent. The candy girl came out, carrying her tray, looking around. She saw

Frankie and stood still, biting her lower lip. Her eyes shone, brightly, wet with the wind.

"Roy, go get us a pretzel."

"Yes, sir."

"Make sure it's warm."

"I know."

Roy watched Frankie go to her, lean into her, talking. She looked nervous, like a horse that's been spooked too many times and is always worried, always ready to kick, to run. They stood close together, both of them looking cold, and Roy thought they looked like they had known each other forever. A lantern fell from its line. The flame crashed high into the air, the hot, twitching light moving over the faces around him. Red light danced in the sky. Roy's breath steamed thickly and Frankie took his hand, hard, pulling.

"Let's go."

They left the show. Roy looked back at the girl, but her thin back was to him. The policemen were talking to her, stooped over her, snow building on their hats. They smiled pleasantly, formally, like they hand learned it from a book. When she turned her head, hiding from them behind her hair, Roy saw she was smiling. Two roughnecks ran past her and threw sand on the small fire. A boy screamed happily as the flames bit into a bale of hay and ran toward a tent.

Roy woke before dawn. They had stopped driving, so the car was cold. Snow covered the windscreen and had built up on the side windows, catching the moonlight. He looked over at Frankie, laying back, his neck still straight, asleep. His brow was creased and Roy thought Frankie had to force his eyes closed, to force himself to sleep. A dim line of moonlight came through Frankie's window and made his skin look frozen, like ceramic. Roy listened to the spare traffic off the highway, to the heavy sigh of lonesome trucks on morning runs. He felt Frankie wake up, put a cigarette in his mouth, and turn the ignition to start the heater. Frankie switched on the windshield wipers and the snow fell away from the car.

The show was closed. The heavy gates were locked with a chain and behind them the once colorful tents sagged, worn and faded by the sky and the snow. A sign called them Kentucky's best, showed the human cannonball and an elephant, a rust stain running down his back. Pale snow fell on the clear windscreen. They had been gone a while, Roy thought.

Frankie pushed in the lighter and sat back, waiting for it to pop. He opened his window an inch and the winter air felt good on Roy's face. Frankie lit his cigarette, started the engine, and turned onto the highway. Snow blew thinly away from the car. A dim, pink mist of morning light lined the edge of the sky.

"Where we going?" Roy asked.

"Texas," Frankie said. "I hear there's a hell of a show in Texas."

Enough for a Stranger

This was before the hurricane, before 9/11 even, when people still worried the Quarter was becoming too gentrified, never mind other parts. Summer was longer, hotter, and quieter then. When I go back now it's all too loud, too bright and I leave as soon as I can.

They lived in the front apartment that looked over Esplanade Avenue but the boys made good use of the over-grown courtyard in the back where my stoop sat for the sitting and come night I lay in my chair outside, the air ripe with rotting plantains and my own sweat, and I listened to one of them, the smallest by far, practice clarinet. On a good day he could have been playing with the best of them, that thick, haunted sound wailed through the air, over his mother's old rhythm and blues music. Not many kids were still in love with Dixieland music. But he played everything in a minor key.

Some nights I would lie in bed, sweating and staring at the slow-moving, useless ceiling fan that turned above me, threatening to fall from its sockets and on a bad night threatening to tear the skin from my face, and I would listen for the safe sounds of those boys in bed, still awake and talking though the oldest one tried to get them to be quiet. And I waited for the small one to laugh. It was a stupid sounding donkey laugh that was much too loud but it made me smile.

And far into the night, sometimes so far that the sky was glowing with coming light, I would hear the mother come in the front door, the wall behind my bed backed onto the hallway, I would hear her hard-heeled shoes on the wood floors she kept so clean as she moved through her apartment, and I would pray for a few hours of black sleep.

Lee came by and brought root beer and vanilla ice cream. I made a float for myself and gave him a glass of root beer with ice and he stood in my apartment and looked around. There wasn't much to look around at.

"You look skinny," I said. We sat in the garden chairs by the steps to my apartment and I ate my ice cream float with a long-handled spoon. Though the sky was gray it was still hot and I could feel the coming rain in the heavy air. I took off my shirt and used it to mop sweat from my chest and face and draped it over the back of the chair. "I said you look skinny."

"I heard."

"You eating?"

"I'm alive, ain't I?"

"I guess." I heard them come home, the sounds traveled fast and easy down the courtyard and soon I could smell that espresso coffee she always made.

"Still wearing them ugly shirts," Lee said. He nodded to the flower-print shirt hanging on my chair.

"Your mother liked them."

"Doesn't make them pretty."

"How is she anyway?" I asked.

"Mom? I don't know." He squinted at nothing but the elephant leaves in the garden. "Been a while since we spoke. You heard from her?"

"Not in a long time."

"You two ever make up?" he asked.

"I don't know. She didn't tell me."

He laughed.

My ice cream melted into the root beer and I sipped at it.

"Damn, what's that smell?" Lee looked around.

"I think something died in there," I nodded to the tangle of bush and weeds. "I had a look but couldn't find anything. How's that girl you were seeing?"

"Macy?"

"If you say so."

"Gone."

"Why?"

"Either money or root beer."

"How's that work?" I asked.

"She was upset I didn't have more money. So, when we fought about it she wouldn't stop screaming and I threw my root beer at her. She walked out. I don't know what made her more angry."

I shook my head and waited. I had been wondering how he would bring money up.

"Lost my job," he said. The wind blew somewhere over the tops of the damp brick walls of the courtyard. "Wish I could get disability like you got."

"You don't want what I got."

"I don't guess you might be able to give me a loan?" he asked. "For old times sake?"

I leaned over and took my wallet from my back pocket. "I can give you twenty-five," I said.

"How much you got left?"

"Five. I need milk." I gave him the cash. His hands were damp and even his fingers looked skinny. "If you put that in your arm I'll kill you."

I sat back and waited for him to feel like a decent amount of time had lapsed and he could leave. In the front apartment I could hear the mother talking at one of the boys and I heard that lovely lost sound of the small boy's clarinet playing "Wolverine Blues."

Lee got up to leave. "I wouldn't do that, you know. I wouldn't put it in my arm."
"And I wouldn't kill you." I smiled up at him.

It still hadn't rained but I could feel it getting closer and closer and I came in the side gate and craned my neck as I walked along outside their apartment and tried to see in the windows. It was a nice place, big and clean but empty, without much furniture or much of anything to make it a home. Lining the walls were stacks of books I never saw anyone reading and I brought my head back down and out of their windows as I came to the small porch at the back of their place. She was sitting in the doorway, her blonde bob so freshly bleached that I could smell it.

"Hi, neighbor," I said.

She smiled at me tight-lipped and crossed her arms, holding her shoulders.

"Waiting for the rain?" I asked.

"Yeah. I hope it rains hard." She looked at me and I felt like I was meant to be hitting on her.

"I live in the back," I said. "What's your name?"

"Beth. You?"

I told her my name and she nodded and waited and I wanted to yell at her or laugh at her but I didn't know which. I wanted her to know I wasn't going to be hitting on her any time soon.

"Where the boys at today?" I asked.

"School."

"Oh. Right. That's good." I looked down the lane at the line of palms and giant elephant leaves. I could smell the rotting plantains and the rotting flesh. "I don't know if you can smell it, but something died in here. If one of your boys wants to make five bucks, I could use help finding it and getting rid of it."

"Is that what the smell is?"

"That or I need to shower more."
"Bunny might want the money."
"Bunny?"
"He's the youngest."
"The clarinet?"
"Yes."
"He's talented."
"Thank you." She took my comment for herself.

I looked at her and wanted to point out that I hadn't complimented her but I smiled and started back for my place. I had to hold my breath until I was inside.

That night I heard the boys yelling about the smell but none of them came to my door offering to help. I had trouble sleeping and in the early morning the soft gold light came to the windows and I got out of bed and went looking through the garden and found the cat, fat and bloated and old and he had leaked into the soil. I got rid of the cat and the soil both and took the longest shower but that smell didn't leave my nose for days, until the rain came, hard and heavy and flooding the courtyard, and I spent almost the whole day in a hot bath full of Epsom salts and I finally slept and the only thing I could hear was the rain.

I saw him in the door of a bar sitting on his clarinet case. There was a band playing inside and he watched them vacantly and his thick dark hair twitched in the wind and he looked irritated. I stood next to him and leaned in the doorjamb and smelled the canned air that rushed out of the open doorway. The band was more interested in telling bad jokes than playing music but it was too hot to play, even in the air conditioning, and I saw the beaded sweat on most all of their brows while they stood on stage and worked up the energy to play another song. Sweat ran down my own back and all my clothes clung worse than the most needy of my girlfriends and I looked inside at the bar. There were a few stools right by the air conditioner.

"You want a Coke?" I asked the boy.

He looked up at me. He was either angry or concentrating and his black eyes looked like they would set me on fire.

"There's two stools under the AC there," I pointed. "A coke's yours if you want it."

He blinked at me, trying to place me.

"No thanks, stranger." he said. I liked the way he said stranger, it made him seem like a gangster, or maybe John Wayne.

"Stranger, huh?" I laughed. "I live in the back, by your garden. You know me well enough."

He looked at me, nodding slowly. "Enough for a stranger, I suppose." He stood and picked up his clarinet and I followed him to the bar and asked for a Coke and a root beer.

The band wheezed lazily through another song. They seemed to drag it on too long and then stop abruptly.

"You actually like this music?" I asked.

"Not really," he said.

"Then why we here?"

He held up his cup. "My mom doesn't let me drink Coke."

"Shit."

"Tell me about it. She likes me to drink milk but when it's this hot it just sits and goes sour in my stomach."

"What does she drink?"

"In the day? Coffee."

"And at night?" I asked.

"Sour mash. I don't know what that is."

"It's bourbon. A type of whiskey."

"Ok." He got off the stool and picked up his clarinet and held out his hand. "I have to go home, so thank you for the Coke."

"I've heard these jokes before," I said. "Home time for me too."

We went outside into the heat and everything seemed to slow right down but it may have just been my head. I started to sweat right away.

"So what kind of name is Bunny?" I asked.

"A pretty awful one."

"Yeah, it is. What's your real name?"

"Toby. It's not much better."

"But it is a little better."

"Suppose so."

"Your brothers have idiotic names as well?"

"No."

"Why's that?"

"You got me." He smiled to himself. "Could have called them Cain and Abel."

"They fight a lot?"

"Can't you hear it?"

"Mostly I hear your mother."

We hit Esplanade Ave and turned toward home. The trees hung thick and heavy as though it were too hot for them to grow properly toward the sky and the humidity was such that I thought it might rain again and I hoped so. I slept well in the rain if it came down hard enough.

"What's your name anyway?" he asked.

"They call me Mr. Tibbs."

"Mr. Tibbs?"

"It's a joke."

He looked at me and frowned. "That's a really bad joke."

"Yeah, I know." I saw Lee standing at the side gate. His back was to us and he was sweating badly, his shirt soaked through down the spine. "You got keys for the front door right?" I asked the boy.

"Of course."

"Good. Head on in." I walked faster and hoped Lee wouldn't turn around to me but he did and he smiled and I didn't like it.

When the banging started I was awake but I didn't want to be. It was too early. The air was still cool, that small reprieve from the heat and humidity for the few awake in the hours before dawn was just coming to an end and my head was quiet and my skin was dry and I lay in bed looking at the soft blue sky and tried not to hear her hitting my door. She hit it so hard my floors shook. She called out to me and I stood, holding my head, wishing it were quiet again. I put on a pair of pants and opened the door.

"Morning, Beth." I looked down and the boy was standing in the courtyard behind her. "Bunny."

"Our clothes are gone," she said.

"What?"

"Our clothes are gone. All of them. We had them in the dryer in the laundry room and they are gone."

"And?"

"They were there last night," she said. She was worried and I almost felt bad for her. "No one else would have come downstairs to do their laundry in the middle of the night."

"If you think I took them you can check my place." I stood back. She leaned forward to look inside and her eyes went to the prescription bottles on my bedside table. There wasn't much else to see anyway, just some old LPs next to the player on the floor and I looked into my own room and it was bright with the soft gray morning light and dusty and it didn't look like any place of mine. I wouldn't let things get so dusty. And where the hell was my television? It had been gone a while but I couldn't think of when.

She was still talking.

"Sorry," I said. "I'm still waking up. Say that again?"

"I saw that friend of yours here last night."

"Lee?"

"I don't know his name. The skinny blond boy."

"Yeah, that's Lee." I nodded. "He doesn't live far. Just in the Bywater. I'll go check his place now." I took a shirt from the closet and put on my sandals. "You want to come?" I looked at her. She was pretty. Almost as pretty as she thought she was.

"Bunny will go with you," she said.

I nodded and started out. I heard Bunny's steps behind me and I could feel her looking at me, standing by my open door and I walked down the side and onto the street and hoped she would close my door.

Bunny caught up once we were on the street and he didn't say anything. I looked down at him and he still had sleep on his face and we turned over into the Bywater and the houses became smaller and more run down, little shotgun houses in bad need of a new coat of paint, but they were quiet in the way of early morning when everyone is asleep and you can almost hear the insomniacs thinking about how nice it would be if they could have just one hour rest.

The boy was so small he had to walk quickly to keep up with me and I could feel his embarrassment.

"Lee can be a bit of a pain," I said.

"Did he take our clothes?"

"He might not have known what he was doing. He's a little out of it sometimes. He probably thought they were his clothes."

"None of them will fit."

"No, I don't guess they will."

"Why would he think they were his?"

I shrugged. We came to Lee's house and I knocked on the door. The sound was far too loud in the hush of morning and I stopped and tried the handle. It was open. "Hold your breath, kid."

"Really?"

"Maybe."

We went in and it was dark, the vague shaft of light from the front door the only thing to see by and I left it open. All his shutters were closed and the house was stuffy and stale and had that horrible smell, some bad mix of mildew and nihilism that I shouldn't have known. It was a mess. Not in any scattered or lazy way that may lend itself a certain charm but just plain awful. Bottles of booze, wet, mashed out cigarettes in coffee cups and no sign of food, which may have been a blessing, and a pile of dark clothes on the sofa.

"Those yours?" I asked.

Bunny walked in carefully. "Some." He held up a shirt. "This isn't but those are my brother's school pants."

I went to the kitchen and got him a black garbage bag from under the sink. There was a rubber tube and a burnt spoon on the countertop and I looked at them and went back to Bunny.

"Go through the pile and put your stuff in the bag. Be fast."

"This place looks like a junkyard."

"More than you know."

I left the boy alone and went into Lee's bedroom. He lay on the bed and his eyes fluttered when I shut the door behind me but he stayed sleeping. Or whatever. I sat next to him on the bed and felt sick. There was another rubber tube on the floor next to him and I wondered where they got those things.

I picked it up and pulled at it and I wrapped it around Lee's neck. I tied it tight and when he forced his eyes open, I pulled it tighter and saw the veins in his neck bulge up. He sputtered and tried to take my arm in his hands but he couldn't lift them and he gave up. I listened to him choke and I tried to smile calmly at him, to tell him not to worry. His face was almost purple and he kept opening and closing his mouth, hoping for air but the tube was too tight around his throat and he got nothing.

I untied the tube and put it under the bed and placed my ear by Lee's mouth until I heard the soft rasp of his breath.

Bunny had two bags of clothes and I took one and we left the house. It was still quiet out, still cool but the wind was heavy in a way that promised severe heat for the coming day and I was glad when we got back to the trees of Esplanade Ave.

"Is Lee your son?" the boy asked.

"Sort of." We passed the corner store and it had just opened. "You want an ice cream float?"

"What's that?"

"You don't know what an ice cream float is?"

"No."

"Put two scoops of vanilla ice cream in a big glass and top it with root beer. There's nothing like it."

"Okay."

We got back with the laundry and a bag with ice cream and two bottles of root beer. Bunny went inside his apartment and I sat in the back courtyard and waited for the rain but it never came.

I saw them in the square and I waved and the boys smiled back at me but she just gave me a look and crossed her legs and I walked into the cathedral thinking some things I shouldn't have thought in any cathedral but sitting in the cool dark listening to the ramblings of some crazy Catholic I started to smile, thinking of the way the three boys always ambled and bumped around, like half-wit puppies. I stayed in the cathedral longer than usual, time running away on me again, and, when I came out, it was dark and there was such a crowd around the band I couldn't have seen them if I wanted to.

It stayed hot and the air smelled like rain but it was only a tease and none came, not for days, maybe weeks and I sat in the courtyard eating ice cream and sweating and staring at the red brick walls thinking the dampness in them made them look like they were bleeding but inanimate objects couldn't get stigmata.

And at night I heard him play clarinet. Warm sounds from a pure belly that came through the walls and the occasional squeak and when he tried to bebop things up I heard his brothers call it farting and laugh at him.

I stood on their porch and knocked on the door. I knew she had just woken up because the Greek music she listened to every morning had started half an hour ago and I moved closer to the door, into the shade, as she opened it and nearly bumped my head on hers. She looked scared of me. I never thought of myself as scary looking, never thought there was a single frightful thing about me.

"Morning, Beth."

"Hey."

I held up the paper grocery bag. "It's supposed to go over a hundred degrees today," I said. "So I picked up some ice cream and stuff so the boys could have some floats."

"Sorry, they aren't allowed to eat junk food."

"Oh, this can't count," I said. "It'll be too darned hot today to not have something like this. The ice cream is made with real milk."

"That's too much sugar for them."

"You sure?" I asked.

Bunny came up behind her with one of his brothers. His brother was a good head taller than him but I didn't think much older.

"Floats?" Bunny asked.

"No," she said.

I wanted to tell her I wasn't looking for a way in. I wasn't looking for anything. I Iell, I didn't want a damn thing to do with her but to give her ice cream for her kids.

"Okay," I smiled. "Stay in the shade today. It's gonna be a killer."

I ate the ice cream in the courtyard and thought about going to church to hide from the heat and that steaming sun but by the time night fell I still hadn't come to a decision.

"King Porter Stomp" was always one of my favorites but he was new to it and had torn it to pieces and when he went wrong he played with the sounds and always in a haunting, lonesome way and sitting in the courtyard with the sun warm and wet above me I still got a shiver. I looked in at my place and it was empty and clean and I had even cleaned the wood floors so they shone golden, like solid honey, almost as good as the floors up the front. But that place was wide open, always breezy and bright. Mine looked more like a cool cave perfect for some nesting nightmare.

I went into my kitchen and poured the last of the root beer into a plastic cup and added ice. I had no ice cream left. Through the thin walls I could hear Bunny turning the Stomp into a funeral march and I thought for such a smiling, laughing boy he sure liked his melancholy. I went back outside and shut the door to my apartment behind me.

I sat in one of the plastic garden chairs and drank the root beer while he played his clarinet and I thumbed through the box of LPs that sat on the ground at my feet. I couldn't find the one I wanted.

Bunny stopped playing and I got up and carried the box of LPs down the side courtyard and I looked through the open back door and he saw me and came out.

"You moving?" he asked.

"Yeah."

"Where to?"

"I haven't decided yet. Either east to Pensacola or west to Gavelstone."

"Leaving town? I thought you were just moving to a new home."

I looked past him into the apartment but I didn't see his mother. "No, I need some distance. I need a change."

"From what?"

"God knows," I said. The box of LPs was getting heavy and the steamy air turned to sweat on my skin.

"Don't think I could ever live anywhere else," he said.
"Pretty young to decide that."
"Maybe."
"Where's your mother at?" I asked.
"She didn't come home yet."
"Your brothers?"
"They went to school."
"You didn't?"
"Not 'til mom comes home." He smiled.
"Come out to my car a minute."
I got that look from him. "What for?" he asked.
"I want to give you something." I started down to the side gate. "I think you'll like it."

He thought for a second and then I heard him walking behind me.

I opened my trunk but there was no room for the box in my hands.

"Open that back door for me?" I asked. He did and I put the box inside and went back to the trunk. I started to flip through a milk crate with more records. "This is the first time in close to ten years that I actually have these things in any order. Mostly they stay scattered in a midnight mess on my floor and I pretend I know where they're at." I found the record I was after and I wiped it clean with the tail of my shirt. "Yours," I said.

He took it and read the label. *Mournful Serenade?*
"You'll like it."
"If you say so." He held out his hand to me and I shook it. He had a firm dry grip and I knew my own hand would be clammy, rubbery with over-medicated bones and I wondered how I would sleep now and what would I listen to when I lay in the dark.

Innocent

The first time she came north she was six but looked younger. Richard waited outside the station until he saw the train come through the clouds and slow into the tunnel and he went inside and stood by the beaten looking oak doors. The ticket teller watched him, smiled at him. Richard stared until the teller looked away, and he tried to breathe, tried to unwind, and went out to the train and saw her standing on the platform. She was small and dark and he thought she looked dim, something slow and bovine in her eyes he didn't like.

He waved to her and she came over. The train sighed loudly and he smelled the burnt oil. He looked down at her and thought she should be taller, less baby-looking.

"You remember me?" he asked.

"No."

"But you know who I am."

"Yes. Richard."

He shook his head and thought he could have been anybody. "Now I know my name, you ready to go?"

"I don't know where my bags are."

"Where'd you put them last?"

"I don't know." Her breath misted slightly and she watched it. "I'm cold. It's May, it should be summer."

"The ice is still in the mountains. It's still melting. It'll warm up soon enough."

She nodded and looked at a baggage cart being pushed along the platform. The cold air came hard through the tunnel, clean and northern, and Richard smiled down at his daughter and knew what her mother would have told her. He shrugged.

"Your bag on the cart, there?"

"Yeah."

"Go get it."

She watched the mountains while he drove, her window down, the air coming in fast and sharp and he told her soon the hills around them would be bright, flaming and red with fireweed. Her head stayed turned away from him, her hair floating out behind her, but she nodded. The sun hung low and lonesome-looking and burnt softly, like cooked honey, in the pale, empty sky.

She unpacked her bags and came out on the porch and he looked at her, realized there was no place for her to sit, no second chair. He remembered how thoughtful she had looked as a baby and wondered what happened. She sat on the floor with her back to the wall. Soot spread onto her shirt.

"We'll have to get you some other clothes."

"Okay." She squinted. He tried to think who she looked like. No one he knew. "It that a lake over there?"

"Yes."

"It looks big."

"It is." The evening came on cold though the sun stayed in the sky, stayed soft, down in the trees and she sat quietly while he watched her. "What do you like to do?" he asked.

She shrugged. "Play with friends? Watch TV?"

"I don't have one."

"A friend?"

"A TV."

"That's okay."

She had been a demanding baby, spoiled by her mother, and he still saw the ugly look on her face that told him she wasn't getting what she wanted. It was in the cheeks. He smiled at the thought that she was too nervous to speak up.

"We could play with fire?"

She grinned at him, excited and scared, and he started laughing.

It rained for three days and he wanted to kill her. It was the way she sat inside looking at nothing, not doing or saying anything and when he tried to show her how to cook, she walked away, quiet, bored, and he burnt the pork. She sat on the sofa and looked ahead at the window but didn't notice the view, the trees or the cold, wet light. There was nothing in her eyes and that, and the sound of the rain on the roof, set his nerves on edge.

She had liked the fire. She hadn't touched it, hadn't played with it, but let him poke and prod and bring up bursts of sparks, and she smiled and looked him in the eye and he knew she was happy.

"You don't have a TV," she said.

"No. We've been over that."

"It must be nice here when it snows."

"It is."

"Is it very cold?"

"Yes."

"You don't have electric heaters."

"Got a plug in. But it doesn't seem to do much good. I keep the fire going all night."

"Do you have to wake up to give it more wood?"

"Sometimes."

"Mom said you hate waking up."

He smiled and waited for the questions, for the comments. He had been waiting a while, thinking of them for months before she came even, trying to think of answers and not coming up with anything. She turned away from him, her nose small and round and her mouth open as though she were mid-thought and he saw she would be a handsome woman when she was old, not cute or pretty. There was something stone-like and hard to her. Something familiar.

"I can still see the lake."

"Yeah?"

"There's someone on it."

"Should we notify the church?"

"What?"

"If there is someone walking on the water, we should tell them."

"Not walking. In a boat."

Tough crowd, he thought.

"Fishing. In all this rain."

"It's a good time to fish." He smiled.

Later, when the rain stopped, he took her out in the canoe to show her the lake. The air was thick and damp with a cold mist that hung nervously over the water and he watched her, smiling, still surprised he had a daughter, still surprised she came to see him, and he thought thank heaven she doesn't look like her parents. He looked up the hill and saw a gathering of bison, four or five, at the tree line, watching him, their chests swollen and eyes bright. They looked angry.

"Can we fish?" she asked.

"I can."

"Not me?"

"Need to buy you a few things."

"Show me how?"

"Sure."

He tied the line silently and held it out for her to see and she touched the hook with her finger and nodded, focused and happy. She watched him cast and reel in and later, when the air had warmed and softened and made Richard lazy so he got the hook caught in his finger, she watched, wide-eyed and happy, as he cut the hook with pliers and pulled it out, his finger running with blood.

"You like that?" he asked.

"A little."

"We better go in. The sky's going dark again."

"More rain?"

"More rain."

He paddled the canoe and she watched him, her eyes dark and, he thought, not so bovine with the wind strong in her face, but still vacant, waiting and expecting and he turned away and looked at the lake running and rippling as the wind grew.

"What would we have done if we caught one?" she asked.

"A fish? We'd have had it for dinner."

"How?"

"How? We'd cook it."

"So we would kill it first."

"Yes. We'd kill it, gut it and clean it. Then we could cook it."

"Okay." She nodded. "Can you show me that tomorrow?"

"Yes."

She nodded and watched the hills come closer. The rain started; light, delicate rain that came from a deep and windy sky that had fallen down from the mountains, still heavy with ice. It beaded her face and she blinked the water from her eyelashes and looked up at Richard and he thought about how to teach her to kill.

On her last day with him he woke early and went out to the lake and sat alone and wished he still smoked, if only for the company of the fire in his hand. It was warm, the ice gone from the mountains and the wind.

He took her to the train station and they sat at a bench on the platform, waiting for the train, listening to it rumble over the hills, coming closer. There was blood on her jacket and he thought he should have bought her another one for fishing, for killing. He wet his thumb and rubbed at the blood but it was long dry and had set and she shook her head at him for trying.

"I should have got those clothes I kept promising. I'm sorry."

"Next time," she said.

"So you're coming again?"

"Next year. If she lets me."

The train came to a stop and he walked her on board, up to her seat, the air inside dry and foul and hard on his stomach. She sat down and looked out the window.

"Be good, Jodie."

She nodded.

She came again, the following year, later in the summer, after the ice had gone but the mosquitoes were thick, and he saw her standing inside the train station, waiting, and he thought her face was still bland and her eyes were still dull. He wanted to shake her.

"You haven't grown very much," he said. "How's your mother?"

"She's okay. She still doesn't believe you have electricity."

They stayed up late and watched the sun and the sky change color and he told her the sun would go down, but only a little, only for an hour or two, just dipping into the horizon, and the sky would go from pale evening to cold, blue morning without any real night and she said that was crazy, everything up here was crazy.

"Can we go fishing tomorrow?" she asked.

"Sure."

"I've been thinking about that all year. About fishing, I mean."

"Well, I got some things for you. A jacket and some gloves that have a good grip, so you don't have to feel the slime of the fish, or worry about the blood and that getting on your hands."

"I don't mind that."

"Really?"

"It's just blood."

"Always gives me the heebie-jeebies, that gunk on my hands," Richard said. He looked at the lake, shining dimly through the trees. It was a clear, thirsty blue that looked inviting but even at this time of year it was still cold enough to shock the lungs and numb the skin.

"I'm glad you got two chairs out here now," she said. "That floor is hard."

In the morning they went out on the lake. He cupped water in his hands and splashed his face to wake up and she watched him and did the same and he told her she could drink it if she wanted but she shook her head. They caught a pair of whitefish, small ones not much bigger than his hands and he watched his daughter, watched her face as she focused on getting the hook out of the fish's mouth.

"It's in there pretty deep," she said.

"Twist it like a letter J."

"You said that."

"Most people don't listen the first time or two."

She smiled at him, her eyes dark and thoughtful and bright and she held up the hook and the fish flipped out of her hand and back into the water.

"Maybe. Tell me about your stepfather."

"Tell me about you and mom."

"What's she tell you?"

"She says you went crazy."

"What do you think?"

"I think there's nothing wrong with that."

When Jodie was ten he almost didn't recognize her. Her hair had become even darker and hung down to the middle of her back and she was longer and leaner and her jaw was set, her face hardened into a look that kept people on the train from talking to her, from saying what a big girl she was, going all that way on the train, alone. When she saw him at the station, standing at the end of the tunnel, near the open air, she ran up to hug him but stopped short, uncertain.

They went into town for dinner, ate cheeseburgers and onion rings at a throwback restaurant and afterward he sat nervously watching the other clients, their huge waistlines hanging over belts, dull and glassy eyes and pallid cheeks. The music made him dizzy.

"I feel skinny in here."

She looked over her shoulder, into the restaurant, her cheekbones high and cutting out of her soft face. "You are."

"Do you drink coffee yet?"

"No."

"Let's get apple pie or something, takeaway, and go home. I've had the pie here, before, a while ago. It was good."

She ate the pie in the car as he drove north, the windows down, the air quiet, the warm smell of the cinnamon and apples filling the car, making him hungry all over again.

"How long has it been since you ate there?"

"A couple of years, I guess."

"The pie's gone downhill."

In the morning he made coffee and went to wait for her on the porch but she was already there, sitting in the sun, her eyes closed, her mouth wide, thick-lipped and relaxed. He stood in her sun and she smiled. She had circles under her eyes, haunted dark smudges she got from him and not from sleeplessness. There was a box at her feet and she inched it toward him with her toe.

"I got you a present."

"Thank you."

"Don't just look at it, open it."

"I will."

She watched him unwrap the box and he held up the knife and thought it was too big, too sharp, and he wondered how she found something so scary but he winked at her and said thank you, ran his thumb along the tip and thought, Jesus, the thing would kill.

"Will we fish today?" she asked.

"Yes."

"Maybe we can take tents. Stay the night on Matchbox Island."

"That was fun last year."

"Fun for you. My tent fell over in all that rain."

"That's why it was fun. You looked like an idiot snake trying to get out of a canvas bag." He looked out at the lake, down through the woods, and the wind ran cold though it was late in June.

Later, when the air had become soft with summer, and he was tired from paddling, they set up camp on Matchbox Island, and she went to a beaver dam and kept fishing there. He sat back and closed his eyes and heard them. He listened but they came and went, low, grinding voices and he went to watch Jodie on the dam, the sun high behind her.

She caught pike and cut them easily, her hands fast and steady, opened them and took off the heads and threw them far into the water. He put the fish in the pan and watched her over the fire as she wiped the blood from her hands, squinting at the lake. Her hair was in a thick braid behind her and it made her look old.

"You hear them too?" he asked.

"Yeah."

"Can you see them?"

"Not yet."

"I think they're around there." He pointed into the trees, deep in the island. He turned the fish over and closed his eyes against the smoke.

"They're moving pretty fast."

"Let's hope they keep moving."

They sat back against willow trees to eat and he watched her face when the sound of a canoe being dragged onto the land came from behind her and the voices were clear.

"I thought no one ever came here," she said.

"No one ever did."

They were young, the youngest a few years older than Jodie and he stared at her, his mouth open, breathing hard, tired, a .22 rifle tied crossways in his pack. The other two had larger calibers and held them tight and scratched at the thin stubble on their chins. Sweat ran from their foreheads and they looked at each other. They smiled with wet lips and open faces, the sun coming through the trees and into their eyes, making them look sideways at the camp and all three looked at Jodie and then at Richard.

The taller of the two leaned against his hip, "This is our camp."

"Yeah?" Richard set his plate down but didn't stand.

"We booked it."

"It's crown land. Can't book a spot on crown land."

"Well, we always come here." He shifted his rifle in his arms and looked from Richard to Jodie.

"There are plenty of good spots up north," Richard said.

"But this is the one we come to. It's the only island."

"There are other islands."

The boy looked at Jodie, his eyes blanketed, his hand squeezing the barrel of the rifle. His skin shone with the sun and Richard watched his face, watched the mouth move slightly, slowly, nothing coming from it and he thought about the way the boys looked at Jodie and the way she looked back, the look similar to the way she cocked her head at a fish before cutting it open.

Richard nodded and looked out at the lake, thinking, wishing the boys were gone, the world was gone and he stood. "We know other places," he said. "Give us a few minutes to pack up our camp."

They packed their camp quietly while the boys stood, watching, their packs still weighing down their shoulders, their rifles still in hand and the wind blew the smoke from the fire at them, making their eyes water and they blinked it away.

Richard paddled south, toward his house, and watched Jodie in the front of the canoe, paddling hard and when she turned to look at the sun he saw her face set hard, high and angry and he wondered if he'd got it wrong again. The shots echoed over the water, loud and erratic, and he looked at the sky and thought all this damn daylight was making him claustrophobic.

She wanted to learn to shoot, she told him, how to use a rifle, how to kill an animal, something bigger than just a fish and he watched her face and patted his shirt pocket for a cigarette, forgetting it had been so long. Her face had thinned out in the last two years; her cheekbones starting to show high and proud like her mother's, but her eyes were still dark and secretive and, on certain days, after she had spent time alone on the lake, stoic enough to make him nervous.

"You're too young," he told her.

"I'll be thirteen next month."

"Which is too young."

She grunted at him and walked away, off the porch and toward the lake, the sunlight in front of her, making her look like a burnt matchstick. He went inside and looked around, tried to remember if he still had his .22, if he still knew how to use it, and he wondered what he was getting himself into.

She took to shooting most mornings, early, while it was still cold and he was asleep, used to the easy sunlight always at his bedroom window. The sound of the rifle woke him, scared him, and he smiled.

When he went downstairs, she was sitting on the porch.

"It's harder than I thought," she said.

"What are you hitting?"

"Nothing."

"What are you trying to hit?"

"Rabbits."

"They've been at running longer than you've been at hunting."

"I guess."

"Try targets. For a year or two, try targets."

She smiled. "You just don't want me gutting anything."

"It makes me queasy."

"You're such a girl."

He laughed and nodded and said he preferred his meat in a package, the cuts already made.

"Let's go camping," he said.

"I'm sick of Matchbox Island."

"We can go up there, in the low mountains."

"We don't have to worry about bears or anything?"

"Better. We don't have to worry about people."

She took the .22 with them, held it at arms until he made her roll it in a blanket on her back and when they stopped for lunch he showed her how to breathe with the rifle. She still missed every shot and he nodded, happy she wasn't any good yet.

He made a small fire and she looked up at the mountains.

"They look far away," she said.

"They are."

"We walking the whole way?"

"Unless you learned how to fly."

"How long will it take?"

"About two days."

"I hope it's a good site."

"It is." He waited for her to say it was too far, the walk was too hard and he watched her face for the sour softness that crept into her on the bad days. She took a canteen from her bag and had a sip. The water ran down her chin and she held the bottle out to him.

"Mom told me you used to drink a lot."

"I did."

"Were you an alcoholic?"

"I think so."

"What was it?"

"Potato juice."

"No, what was it that made you drink so much?"

"People, I guess. Too many people. It made me feel like flies were crawling in my ears, down my throat."

"Not many people up here," she said.

"No, but there sure are a lot of flies."

She frowned at the clouds, dark and rolling gently toward the mountains, pushed by a softly crying wind and she looked back at him. "What the hell is potato juice?"

They walked for two days and set up camp at the foot of the mountain range, their tents dark on the bright pink field of fireweed and he lay back and watched the mountains split the clouds while Jodie got dinner ready. He thought about her mother, about the flies he had once felt, the crawling of his skin, and he looked around, looked up at the mountains and breathed, tried to unwind, his stomach tight just at the thought. When she started a campfire, the smoke came right at him. His eyes watered.

Jodie looked down at him. "You crying?"

"No."

"Good."

They ate dinner and she watched the sky. Richard thought she was wishing for nightfall. A cool, dry wind blew and sparked the fire, made it burn and glow, the embers showing like a Cheshire cat's grin and he listened to the wood pop and fall into ash.

"We going to stay here a few days?" she asked.

"If you like."

"It's a good spot. I can hear a river, I think."

"It's over there. Plenty of salmon."

She nodded and looked up at the mountains again. "I kind of want to keep going."

"We can do that."

"Can we go up the mountain?"

"We might have to go around."

"That'll do." She stood up, emptied her tea into the side of the fire and looked around. Stray hairs blew slowly in the wind and she was long and lean and dark. She frowned and turned away.

She said good night and went into her tent.

It was cold when she shook him awake and said they should get started, it might rain later and she wanted to cover ground.

"Rain?"

"Yes," she said. "I can smell it."

"Maybe it's the river."

"No. I can smell that too."

"We'll need food. We have to stay with the river."

"So long as we get going."

"What's the rush?"

"I told you. Rain."

He got up and looked at the sky, then back at her and thought, no, it was something else. She had made oatmeal and coffee and was eating already, her face thoughtful, the rifle leaning on her knee. He washed his face with water from his canteen. Cleared his eyes and pushed his hair from his face. The sky was cold, neon blue and electric as ice, but the air was dry and he didn't think it would rain for days.

They stopped at the riverside. It was late, and the sky was soft, dusty with the sun gone, seemingly back south, hiding, just for an hour or two. The pink clouds turned to a thin mist and spread over the land like watered-down blood and Richard went to the river and washed his face and sat a moment, cool and wet, before stripping down to his shorts and getting in. He saw Jodie watching him, worried, a tent pole in her hand. He gave her a thumbs-up and stayed close to the bank. He felt a stone cut his foot and fell back, sank into the water, felt the current pulling at him though it was only shin deep. He closed his eyes and thought thank god, and he remembered the look Jodie's mother had given him. Anyone would need to get away from that.

He jumped when she started shooting. She fired five, maybe six times and he was beside her, dripping, cold, scared as all hell. The air was burnt through with gunpowder and she was smiling, wolf-like and out of the corner of her mouth.

He looked where she had been shooting. "What the hell?"

"I thought I saw something."

"What kind of something."

"I don't know." She turned and looked at the mountains, her skin dark against the sky. "Maybe it was just those flies of yours."

He stood, still dripping, still cold, watching his daughter, watching her eyes, and he thought they had gone darker every year so that now they looked black enough to be holding some kind of fire. Something ran in the woods and she raised an eyebrow at him.

"Not the flies then," she said.

"Sure." But he thought no, the panic, the claustrophobia, the choking down of the flies, was still all over her face, a tell-tale darkness under the eyes, a stoic stillness in the turned lip. She couldn't breathe until she looked up at the open, empty mountains and he knew it.

She stayed longer the next year and longer still, nearly the whole summer, when she was fifteen, and he watched as age and solitude bred a disquiet in her that he was accustomed to.

At fifteen she was almost as tall as he, and she was thin and hardened, but he still remembered the breakable baby she had been for so long, years even, spoiled and soft, with a poisonous selfish streak he suspected still slithered under her skin.

"They're starting in on me with the university thing," she said.

"Who?"

"Mom and dad."

"Oh." He drove west, the land quiet around him, the small herds of buffalo spotting the hills. He wondered what it was like when there were thousands. "What's the university thing mean?"

"Getting me to pick one, to pick a major."

"Oh."

"Did you go?"

"To university? Yes. That's where I met your mother."

"I didn't know that."

"But I never finished."

"What did you study?"

"Political science."

"Really?" She looked at him, smiling.

"Yes."

"Sure wouldn't have seen that coming." She sipped at gas station coffee they had bought earlier and he thought it must be cold by now but it didn't matter, with all the sugar she used it would be like soda anyway. "Why didn't you finish?"

"Didn't like it too much."

"Why?"

"Lot of people in those classes, all talking, flirting and flitting, the whole campus buzzing with people all the time."

"Buzzing like those flies of yours."

"I guess."
"What did you do when you left?"
"Spent some time in a sanatorium."
"What's that?"
"A safe place."
"Like here?"
"I guess. What's your mom told you?"
"Less and less."

He pulled the car over and said that was as far as it would go, they would walk to the river and keep going in the canoe.

"Where are we?"
"Far enough there aren't any names."
"The river have a name?"
"It does, but I'm in denial."
"Nothing wrong with that."

They paddled the river for six days, stopping for only a few hours to rest, to sleep a little, here and there, when they were tired, when they couldn't go on, the constant summer sun burning brightly, and, he thought, making them stronger. She stopped speaking and, by and by, he knew she was forgetting he was there, with her, behind her, paddling, and when they ate she watched the land or the fire and didn't look at him and he knew she didn't want to and he smiled at the thought.

When they stopped by a lake, when Richard was tired and needed to rest, for more than just hours, she made dinner and looked at the water, following the movement as the lake ran back into another river and she said she wanted to keep going, further, alone, and she would come back for him in four or five days.

"I'll leave you the food," she said.

He shook his head and pointed to the lake and said it was like an all-you-can-eat buffet.

After a week Richard thought he was starting to smell and he took to bathing quickly in the lake, cold as it was, cold enough that his lungs seized up and he was sure his blood froze for a minute, and he washed out his clothes and hung them on a cord to dry in the sunlight. Sometimes he watched the mouth of the river, the water twisting away to the west, hidden in the land, at the far end of the lake. The water ran fast, smooth and vibrant as the silk emerald gown he had seen on a woman once, when he was young, and his mother took him to the circus. Sometimes, when the light was right, he could see into the water, see how shallow it was, see how strong the current was. Strong enough to snap his old bones.

In the few soft-sky hours of lilac dusk he slept, his tent open, the Arctic wind fresh on his cheeks and bare chest, and he heard the movement of the land outside, something stepping softly around the tent.

He saw the paw prints and wondered how long it had stood there, watching him. They were afraid of everything, he thought, a man could live his whole life up here and never see one, but after a week, maybe more, after it had watched him sleep once again, and the paw prints became a regular around the campsite, he saw it on the other side of the lake, at the water, watching him carefully, its face gray, thoughtful, the heavy whiskers twitching when the wind ran. It turned and walked away, heavy, strong, with that peculiar strut of the feline and he didn't see it, or any new prints, again.

At night, when the wind ran colder, ran south, fast, as though looking for the dark, he watched the fire, watched the smoked flames licking and biting, twisting and catching a piece of wood, and he tried to remember how long he had been there, how long she had been gone and he thought it hadn't been long enough.

Cracked Bells

Sig came back to town in October. Most years he was gone all winter. It was a good way to live if you could manage. Get the hell out before the cold came and the night-time settled in for a month. Snow just everywhere. October was pretty, though. Cold enough to quiet the streets and the sky was still bright and clear. When I saw Sig come out of the Copper Corner, he was holding his boots in one hand and lighting a cigarette with the other, smiling back into the bar at someone. I thought maybe it was Erin. She'd kick him out for not wearing his boots and he'd leave rather than put them on. Go and drink on the corner. Smile at the women walking by and make them think twice about how their life was going.

    I stopped at the corner and waited. I didn't want to see him, didn't want to talk to him. I never knew what the hell to say. I don't think he did either but that never stopped him talking. He walked away, on down toward Front Street, cigarette smoke curling out thickly behind him, only wearing his jeans and a thin, faded green work shirt and the wind cracked through the trees, cold and hard, but he didn't notice. It was going to get cold soon, I thought. Already the nights were dropping toward zero.

    The way he smoked that cigarette made me want one. When he was gone, out of sight somewhere near the river,

I crossed the street and went into the Copper Corner. Erin grinned at me like she had some joke she was keeping to herself. She looked good enough to make me nervous and I sat down at the bar and remembered last year, when we got together for a few weeks. Even after all that I was still nervous around her and she knew it. I think she liked it too. And I was nervous because she was only twenty and with almost as many years between us there was some kind of responsibility to it that worried me.

She brought over a bottle of Bud and opened it. "You see Sig?"

I nodded.

"He looked good."

I nodded again and took my beer over to the telephone booth near the pool table. Benny was sitting at the back table. He might have been sleeping. His gray hair was long again and fell across his face but I nodded to him anyway. Erin kept loading the beer fridge and the bottles clinked into each other, the sound loud in the empty bar. She looked up at me. She wasn't laughing at me anymore.

I called my mom and when she answered I took a drink. "Sig's back," I said.

She was quiet for a minute. "In October?"

My father came north when he was fourteen and met my mother. She was married at the time and once she told me they both had things to get away from but I didn't know what she meant. I never heard about what made him move up. When I was little, about seven or eight, he used to take me out to Winter Lake and we'd spend a few days out there, checking the water, and he'd tell me about the dreams he used to have as a kid. He called them visions but I think he meant the same thing. There was always a lot of gold involved, gold that no one had found yet. So, of course, I thought that was why he had moved. When he used pebbles to show me what gold was worth in weight, I thought it made sense, gold was the kind of thing to move for. Years later, when he had gone away for a while, my mother mentioned the limp and the blank spells that he had arrived with. I thought they were from rodeoing, but my mother told me, no, he had had them long before he ever got on a horse, before she met him even.

They met at the Copper Corner, too. My mother had been tending bar there for nearly ten years when my father came in asking for whiskey and she had to kick him out for being underage and he told her that was fine, he would leave, so long as she came with him. And she did. She didn't care that he was nearly still a kid and less than a year later I came along.

They had trouble finding a place to live and spent their first year lakeside, sleeping out and checking the water, checking the silt, and come winter they got caught a few times sleeping in hunting cabins that were only used on the weekends and once, just before I was born, they stayed in a farm house that was falling apart and too dangerous to live in because the roof was sagging under the weight of snow and winter, and my father found an old Colt revolver under the floorboards. He had it next to him when they were woken up by the cops and he got sent to jail for a few months, staying so long mostly because no one really knew what to do with him. The gun was stolen and had been used in a murder six years earlier, when he would have been eight. He was still in jail when I was born, but he had found a few small scraps of gold that he had given to my mother and it was enough to get her a place in town and see her through until he was out.

Afterward, a few people let him lie about his age so that he could get work here and there, as a janitor, as a bartender, doing whatever was needed on a ranch or farm. But between the blank spells and his wandering off in the night after another dream he never kept a job long, and, in the end spent too much time lakeside, looking for gold, until someone told him that he could make good prize money jumping off a running horse to bring down a steer. And he was the same with my mother. There one night and gone the next, letting her worry and in the end she realized he was still a kid and she was on her own. Well, on her own with me. I don't know if that made it better or worse.

Like I said, October was good, but even so the cold was creeping in. On weekends, I cut and sold extra wood every year, mostly to friends of my mother's, but I never seemed to get enough to even cover gasoline and a few extra beers. One year I tried just giving the wood away. I thought maybe I could cut and move a little less that way, but most people insisted on paying. Just not enough. But money in the pocket was money in the pocket, even if it was nickels and dimes, and if I didn't buy the permit, I could scrape up something extra. Mostly though, I liked being out there by Willow Creek, when the mornings were cold and crisp, so much so that the air was almost hard against my cheeks. And the fresh cut pine smelled good, too.

I liked to fell the trees with the axe and use the saw after the tree was down. Erin came out with me once when we spent time together. We spent more time kissing than cutting but she still knew that I used the axe because I was afraid to use the chainsaw when the tree was still up. I always thought the tree would come down too fast, too hard and wrong and that I'd get smashed up.

I called my mother in the morning, before heading out. She always woke early and, when Sig was in town, I was sure she slept a little less, worried a little more.

"I'm going out for wood. How low are you?" I asked.

"I'm okay. But load up good anyway. I had a dream last night that it was going to be cold this winter."

"It's cold every winter."

"Extra cold."

I listened. I could hear her Bob Dylan music in the background. "Is Sig there?" I asked.

"No. Why would he be?"

"You got the Bob Dylan on."

"I like Bob Dylan."

"I know."

"Have you seen Sig again?" she asked.

"Not since the other night."

"How'd he look?"

I thought about that. I don't think I saw the same things other people saw when it came to Sig. They saw the smile, the eyes, all that excitement, and all I saw was blue jeans worn so thin he might as well have been wearing cheesecloth. Also, I was the only person that ever saw him sleeping in doorways covered in spilled beer and cigarette ash. It got so that sometimes I thought I was having visions of my own, like my father's gold visions when I was a kid, just not nearly as exciting or worthwhile. I thought about the way Erin had looked at me after she had kicked Sig out of the bar. It made me a little jealous. "Erin said he looked good, so there's that."

"I like Erin."

"Yeah," I said. "She's a good kid."

My mother snorted and hung up.

That day I cut a lot of wood, almost a full cord so there'd be plenty to come back for, and I tried not to think too much about Erin.

I had trouble breathing. It happened sometimes when Sig was around. Just knowing he was back, knowing he was in town, and I had an invisible mask on, thick as a wool sock. I checked on my mother a little more, called her when I could and sometimes drove over to the house when she was off work. If she wasn't home yet I'd wait in the truck, the sky going dark early, looking like winter already. And I stayed away from the Copper Corner and the Buffalo Bar, too, even when I wanted a beer or wanted to see Erin. Sometimes I tried to work out when she'd be on shift, but didn't get anywhere. And a few times I walked by the Copper Corner and looked through the window but I could hear Bob Dylan going and knew Sig was inside.

Most years, when Sig worked his way back up to town, usually before the end of rodeo season, I knew the routine. I knew he'd be around for a month, maybe two, before he got antsy and slipped away. I didn't know what to do about him being around in winter. Soon it would be too cold for him to sleep outside, and I was afraid that my mother would get him to come and stay in the house again.

I was on Steele Street and it was just getting dark. People were leaving work and the lights from the café were starting to look bright when I saw Sig on the library steps. He was sprawled out, his legs stretched and crossed at the ankles, a little too comfortable, and he was singing. Loud. Nursery rhymes and a folk song or two. He never panhandled, never had a hat out or anything, but sometime people gave him money all the same. I didn't see why they would. He didn't need it. When he walked into a bar someone always bought him a beer and he'd come out a few hours later all bleary-eyed and lost. I looked at him over on the steps, singing, nearly shouting, and I wondered how long he had been in the bar that day. Some teenagers walked by, two girls, and Sig started in on Bob Dylan's *I Want You*, and they ignored him, walked a little faster, but when they got near me I saw they were blushing. How could a man like Sig make a pretty young lady blush like that?

I went into the café and got a couple of donuts and coffee and sat down at the window. The two teenagers were in there, too, and one of them kept looking out the window, over at Sig. Once I told Erin that people said he looked like Paul Newman and she told me he looked better but it wasn't that, there was something else people liked about him. Not just women, either. Kids loved him. Half the town went out of their way to buy him a beer.

He stopped singing and stood up, looked down at himself and then his pants went dark and I turned away but couldn't eat my donuts. I wondered why people wanted to buy a beer for a man who wet his pants while standing on the library steps.

That night I went to see my mother. She was tired but it wasn't because of Sig. She told me she just got like that every year, when winter was coming.

"I never noticed before," I said.

"You haven't come around this much before."

"Sure I have."

She smiled and started to heat up some venison chili I had made for her a few days ago and she told me Sig was at it again, that he had watched some kids playing rag tag baseball without any gear and then he'd show up the next day with new gloves and baseball bats and even a hockey mask for the catcher and got the game really going. The kids loved it. Parents too. I didn't tell her that I had seen him wet himself at the library.

My father was always around, at the edges of my life. I think his whereabouts had more to do with his dreams than with me. I stayed with him every now and then, sometimes in the motel out on the highway, near the deer run, sometimes camping near the rivers. Once when we were spending a few days together the temperature dropped real low, cold enough to snow but the sky was all blue and nights were just razors of ice, so we stayed in his car. It smelled of oiled leather and riding gear and it dawned on me, I guess I was eleven or so, that he didn't have a home or apartment or anything.

When he spent too much time down south, working, he'd get anxious. His dreams became few and far between, and what little there was became vague so that he couldn't see the land anymore, and didn't know where to look when he woke up. He told me once it was like drying out until you were just dust.

There was enough to his dreams that people let it be when he mentioned he was going over to Grey Valley or up toward McGill to look for gold. But not enough that he had to worry about anyone following him. He had been working at the Tire Mart for a few months when he gave notice, said Wednesday would be his last day, that he'd leave by lunch, because he wanted to get out before the fire. I guess people just ignored a comment like that but he worked half a day Wednesday and then left, drove down south, and that afternoon there was a fire that took down the whole building and sent two people to the hospital. My mother wasn't at all surprised. Same when he spent a month wintering her house for her, stocking up on wood and just so many cans of beans and filling the freezer because he had a dream about the town being cut off from the world and then that winter the storms got so bad that all the roads south were shut down for a month and most of the town went at least a week without power. Mom let him stay the month with us, on the sofa, but her second husband, Harry, kept giving my father looks that sent him living in the basement and at the end of winter both men moved out. I was pretty happy about that.

When I was twelve I went with him to Red Creek. He told me it would take us at least two weeks looking but that we were sure to come away with three or four ounces of gold. I told him all the gold had been taken a hundred years ago and he looked at me like I was nuts, like I didn't see things quite right but it was okay that way. We made camp in a clearing not far from the river and stayed up late collecting wood and cooking and he told me a little about rodeoing and it was late when a group of girls found us.

There were four of them, in a pair of brand-new bright red canoes, and they asked if they could set up near us and then they brought a flat of beer over when my father and I finished eating dinner and they sat with us for a while. They had a lot of clean hair that smelled good out there in the woods and strong tan legs under long gray sweatshirts. Maybe they were wearing shorts but I couldn't really tell. I kept trying to find out and got caught by one, with wavy hair and big lips and I could see she was really skinny. The kind of skinny I liked, a little like Erin. When she looked hard at me, I went warm, probably went red too, and I hoped it was dark enough that she couldn't see. I guess maybe they were sixteen or seventeen, they were almost done with school and they got excited when my father told them he hadn't ever done much school and it looked like they wanted to wander away as well. Maybe with him. As it got cooler, they seemed to get a little closer to my father and I thought he didn't really look too much older than them but somehow I was stuck still looking like a little kid. One of the girls drank too much and kept putting her hand on my father's leg and he smiled and let it stay and when she leaned over to rest on him, really drunk now, I saw that she had nothing on under her sweatshirt. Nothing at all.

My father let the fire die down and sent me to bed and when I woke he was packing up our camp. He told me he had been up all night, listening to me talk in my sleep about some trees that were a day up-river and still charred from the summer fires. He wanted to check it out. I wanted to stay near those girls, zipped up in their tent and sleeping off the beer, but we got moving and eleven days later we found what turned out to be nearly eight thousand dollars worth of gold. That much money scared my father and he gave it all to my mother and then I didn't see him again for almost a year.

I got a donut at the café. Some early rising workers were in there, getting big cups of coffee to go, dirt and cement on their big yellow boots. They smelled of cigarettes and old wool and had those expensive work jackets on. They made good money. I had worked construction with one or two of the guys years ago but they didn't recognize me. The work season ended soon and they were all worried about that. Saving was hard. Maybe harder than earning. The girl behind the counter gave me an extra donut for free and it made me think about Erin. When she first started working at the Copper Corner she was always coming over with free burgers, telling me Ivan had made an extra by mistake. I thanked the girl for the donut and she smiled at me and I went across the street and looked through the window of the bar. They were closed but it made me feel good to look in there anyway. See where Erin would be standing later on. Benny was in there. Sleeping. Someone had locked him in again. It was easier than waking him up. I wondered if he died would they just leave him sitting there in the back.

    I went out to pick up another load of firewood and filled the truck a little too high so that when I got to the highway and picked up speed, some of it fell off. I left it there for later. The road wasn't used much that time of year.

    It was a good morning, cold and bright, the sun somehow closer than normal. Erin was a morning person. Even working late at the bar she was up by seven, walking around her little place in that long t-shirt she slept in, drinking teas. I don't know how that tea helped her wake up. When we spent time together she'd make me a cup of coffee and sit down on my lap, her shirt riding high, and then smile at me. I think she was laughing at me but I didn't mind. She made terrible coffee but I never told her.

    I was about fifteen minutes out of town, the wood still racking in the back, when I saw Sig. He had an old enamel-looking stove on a flat dolly and was pushing it along the highway. I wanted to turn around. Go back into the woods and come back later, when he was gone. I wondered where the hell he had come from. Where had the stove come from? It was a big thing.

He heard my truck and stopped pushing. Just waited, didn't even turn around. I wondered if he knew it was me. I pulled up alongside him and he grinned at me, took a cigarette out of his pocket and lit it. Even in the cold he was sweating, breathing hard. We were on a bit of a hill, going up. That stove must have weighed the same as my truck.

"What the hell is that?" I asked.

"It's a stove."

"I can see that. Where'd it come from?"

"Bancroft's."

"That quite a ways away."

"Don't I know it."

"You been pushing it all night?"

"Feels like longer."

I sat there in the truck, thinking. Even with the heater broken it was still pretty warm in the cab. And the seats were soft and going uphill didn't feel like anything.

"What the hell you doing with it?" I asked.

"It's for Benny."

"Benny? What's he want with a stove like that?"

"He's got no heating. Why you think he spends all night at the Cop?"

"I didn't know that."

Sig nodded at me.

"Bancroft just give it to you?" I asked.

"I did some work for him."

I looked at the stove and at the dolly. I was surprised it could handle the weight. I was surprised Sig could handle the weight but sometimes he was like cast iron himself.

"That's a lot of wood," he said. "You know you get some side panels you could stack twice as much."

"I don't have the money for side panels."

"Yeah."

I got out of the truck and look in the back. "I don't have any rope," I said.

"Rope?"

"To tow the stove."

"Drop the wood and come back?"

"It's for Marie."

"Oh." Sig nodded. He knew that meant she would talk all day and then I'd have to stick around while she invited mom over and I made us dinner. It would take me forever to get back to him. "Well, I'll just keep pushing."

I shook my head and moved some of the wood around. Took some out and stacked it by the side of the road.

"What are we doing?" Sig asked.

"One of us drives, the other sits back here and sort of holds on to the stove, let it roll along with us."

"Might tear an arm out."

"Then drive slow. I need my arms."

"You got gloves?"

He drove slow and I only dropped the stove twice, when my arms damn near popped out.

I hadn't seen Erin for a couple of days. Not even in the Copper Corner, though I didn't go in, just looked through the window every time I passed. I told myself that maybe that was a good thing. Put some space between us, between my thoughts at least. I saw Sig in there quite a bit though, sitting at the bar, a few people around him, listening. Bob Dylan playing. I used to like Bob Dylan.

One morning I saw Sig sleeping in the door of a real estate office on Steele Street when I was out for a walk. It was early, maybe six and still dark and I could smell frost in the air. I looked down at Sig. There was vomit on his jacket and he had a bruise welled up under his eye. It was still pink.

A broken wine bottle was smashed up in the corner, near his head, the wine dark and smelling and almost frozen. I had the feeling someone threw the bottle at him. Sig was fun but then things turned. People stopped buying drinks and threw them instead. He made a gurgle and I thought about calling my mother, but I didn't want her to worry, or worse yet, get to feeling responsible. I wondered if I should turn him onto his side. Make sure he didn't choke when he puked again, but he rolled over himself, sort of curled up like he was cold and kept sleeping. I shoved five dollars into his pocket and when I went into the café I thought I was pretty stupid. He'd drink it or give it away, thinking he didn't need it. Maybe he was right.

Between seeing Sig and not seeing Erin I decided to stay away from town for a few days and I drove out to Willow Creek and set up camp. I liked it out there. It was the kind of place where the world moved on and didn't care about people. The brush was red and the creek was dark and blue and cold and it was good getting in that water every morning, once the sun was up. I had taken Erin there a couple of times and when she said it was like something out of a dream I laughed and told her she got that right. She found gold too. A real small bit that she just kept. Nearly every time I came out to Willow Creek I found some too. Nothing but thin flakes but I kept mine as well. I thought maybe if we got together again we could put ours together or something. That was the kind of thing she laughed at though. Looked at me like it was her that was twenty years older and I was still a kid.

I spent most mornings sitting in the sun, mapping out some dreams, or in the water and after about a week I was sure Erin would be back at the Copper Corner so I packed up and went into town. I stopped by my mother's first and she told me she'd heard Sig got a job as caretaker at the high school.

"You always said you thought he should go back to school," I said.

"Funny man."

"You think he'll keep the job?" I asked.

"Of course not. He'll be gone in a week or so."

"Even in winter? There's nowhere for him to go."

"He doesn't need somewhere to go, he just needs to go."

I nodded like I knew what she meant and checked her fridge and pantry. She was running low on everything but flour. I wondered if she had given a load to Sig. She wouldn't tell me if she had, though. I wanted to ask her if she had seen Erin around but didn't want to put up with what would come next so I just waited until after six and went into the Copper Corner.

She was there. She almost laughed when she saw me and I pretended not to notice and sat at the bar where I could see her legs. She was wearing some kind of wool skirt and black tights and those shit-kicker boots of hers. When she brought me a beer I looked at her, hard, right in the eye, trying to tell her something but I didn't really know what.

On my third beer Sig came in. He went to the jukebox first and put on *Watchtower*, and came and sat down right next to me. He smelled like he had cleaned himself up and I wondered where he had been staying.

He grinned at me, "Where you been hiding?"

"Under rocks."

He laughed and Erin brought him a whiskey, a double with ice and I thought, oh shit. Erin set the drink down and looked at us, back and forth, side by side, her long hands holding the bar. "Damn, you two look alike sometimes."

Sig just grinned and I told her thanks.

When I was fifteen I had a girlfriend. Mia. We didn't last too long. She told me I wasn't present enough for her and when my father came to town and had a big party for his thirtieth birthday she went off with some rodeo buddy who had given my father a lift. I didn't know what she meant by present. She was the one always itching to leave.

The party was at the Buffalo Bar, before it got fixed up and my father moved back to the Copper Corner, like he suddenly remembered he was old enough that they couldn't kick him out. My mother and I went for a little. We sat in the back, ate overcooked burgers, and my mother watched me draw on a napkin.

People kept on swinging by, setting my father up with another drink, listening for a little. Sometimes he talked about the rodeo. Thirty and he was slowing down. He'd been coming in second and third for a while. If he wanted real money he'd have to start riding the horses, he said, or, and here he'd pause and wink at someone, go back to chasing his dreams. That's where the real money was. People liked that and they liked the way he said it. All friendly. He brought up the find that had happened over at Three Hills, a few years before. He'd had dreams about Three Hills for years but never made it out, and some college kids got there first. Made a killing.

When he said there was always Winter Creek, I wanted to tell him to shut up but it didn't matter because I knew he was blowing hot air. There was nothing at Winter Creek. Not anymore. I thought now he was just making things up. I hoped so. He was on good painkillers from doing his knee in with a steer but when he walked, the limp looked like it was for show.

It got quiet in the bar and my mother got up and went to the jukebox. She was there for a while and I could hear my father, over at the bar, laughing, a good warm laugh that you wanted to hear again and again. The girl behind the bar stayed close. I was pretty used to the look she was giving him. Soon he was telling her about one of his dreams.

Waylon Jennings came over the speakers and my mother came back to the table. She looked at my drawing. I was getting good.

"What you got there?" she asked.

"Just mapping something out."

"Your father used to do that."

I looked at her. It was dark in there but she wasn't smiling. She was looking over at my father, at the bar, talking, trading dreams for drinks.

The snow came early that year. The first week of November. I was near Jackpine, where there was a tear in the hillside and the earth inside was near black and crumbled easily in hand. I couldn't remember how I got there but it didn't matter. I'd find it again easy enough. When I wanted to. But with all the snow and the wind picking up I thought maybe I'd head back to town, stay with my mother for a little, make sure she was fine, give her the three or four hundred dollars' worth of gold I had come across. And I was still worried about Sig. I didn't want him to get stuck in town all winter.

On the way back to town I stopped at Willow Creek. I wanted to load up the truck with more firewood, spend a last night out there, before the real weather came. A couple of trees I had taken down were still there but when I looked around, I had the feeling someone had been there, digging. A few years before I had been hunted by a mountain lion for a couple of days and it felt a little the same. Like waiting for something when you couldn't breathe. I didn't stay the night. Just cut up a bit of extra wood and went to town, wondered *who had been sleeping in my bed?*

The Copper Corner was empty and with all the snow outside and that sense of quiet from the cold night I went in for a beer. A girl I hadn't seen before was behind the bar, wearing a parka. She got my beer from the ice bucket, wiped the ice away and set it down in front of me. Gave me a really big smile. The kind Sig usually got. I wondered where she was from. She had a lip ring and I kept thinking it was going to rip on something but then I realized she thought I was staring at her lips, like I was after something.

As I paid, I asked the new girl when Erin was on next.

"Erin? I think that's who I replaced."

"Replaced?"

She looked at me and grinned, saw right through me and knew what I was worried about. "Sure. She packed up and left town. Last Tuesday. Drove down south with Sig."

"She went with Sig?"

"Yep," she nodded. She tongued her lip. "They're going to a rodeo or something."

"In November? They'd have to go all the way to Texas for a rodeo in November."

The girl shrugged and looked at me. Behind her, on the wall, was an old trophy; nearly two feet of twisted and tarnished silver horse, that Sig won at one of the big rodeos down south, when he first started to compete. It wasn't worth anything but pride, and he still sold it for a bottle of Seagrams.

I took my beer and went to sit with Benny. I wondered why he was still in the bar, now that he had his big stove.

Acknowledgments

Gratefully acknowledged are the following publications, where stories first appeared in earlier versions:

"The Wrong Side of Gone" – *The Southern Review*
"The Luckiest Man in Town" – *Ploughshares*
"All Gone Now" – *Glimmer Train*
"Nothing Shaking" – *The Bellevue Review*
"Clear Midnight" – *The Australian Book Review*
"Mount to the Sky" – *The Saturday Evening Post*
"Some Kind of Heaven" – *The Georgetown Review*
"Muddle Through" – *The Chattahoochee Review*
"Enough for a Stranger" – *The Potomac Review*
"Innocent" – *The New Ohio Review*
"Cracked Bells" – *The Fiddlehead*

Thanks to Gramps, Mom, and Katerina. For everything. And in absolutely no order, a few people who have helped, inspired, influenced—Bob French, Anthony "Tuba Fats" Lacen, Michael Sala, Joanna Pearson, Mark Jarman, The Carter Family (Phil, Lynn and Alex), K. Arthur Guy, Barry Corber, Craig, Jesper, Margaret, Jill, Connell, Michael, Cedric, Farley and John, and Ed Ricketts. Also thanks to my agent Ellen Levine and her team at Trident and, finally, the good people at Cornerstone, notably Dr. Ross Tangedal, Brett Hill, Sam Bjork, Sophie McPherson, and Andrew Bryant.

Finally, thanks to Will Powers.

Michael Caleb Tasker won the 2019 *Saturday Evening Post* Great American Fiction Contest for his story "Mount to the Sky." He has been published in numerous literary journals, including *Ploughshares, Glimmer Train, The Southern Review, Ellery Queen's Mystery Magazine,* and *The Australian Book Review*, and was runner-up in the John Steinbeck award for short fiction. He currently lives in Adelaide, Australia, where he manages a visual arts and supplies building.

www.ingramcontent.com/pod-product-compliance
Lightning Source LLC
LaVergne TN
LVHW040054080526
838202LV00045B/3626